D0160480

The Many Fortunes of Maya

The Many Fortunes of MAYA

★ ★ ★

Nicole D. Collier

▼ VERSIFY
An Imprint of HarperCollins Publishers

Versify® is an imprint of HarperCollins Publishers.

The Many Fortunes of Maya
Copyright © 2022 by Nicole D. Collier
Illustrations © 2022 by Sawyer Cloud
All rights reserved. Printed in the United States of America.
No part of this book may be used or reproduced in any manner
whatsoever without written permission except in the case of
brief quotations embodied in critical articles and reviews. For
information address HarperCollins Children's Books, a division of
HarperCollins Publishers, 195 Broadway, New York, NY 10007.
www.harpercollinschildrens.com

ISBN 978-0-35-843464-1

Typography by Carla Weise
22 23 24 25 26   PC/LSCH   10 9 8 7 6 5 4 3 2 1
First Edition

For Daddy,
my forever Grill Master

CHAPTER 1

☆

Favorite Things

**You have firm convictions—
stand strong behind them.**

Even though I've never seen one in person, wood thrushes are my favorite bird of all time. They sing the perfect summer song. They sound like sunshine and fun and good luck. Whatever mood you're in, if you hear a wood thrush singing, you're gonna feel ten times better, I promise. But they don't come around very often. So when I woke up this morning and heard one, I knew it was my lucky day.

Wood thrushes remind me of my favorite instrument, the flute. Uncle Jimmy taught me to play forever ago, and in the beginning, my flute went everywhere

I did. I loved it so much, I even named her Flicker. Flicker the Flute. Then Daddy taught me soccer, and I loved that, too. But after a while, it was like a seesaw, with soccer on the one side and Flicker on the other. I couldn't do them both at the same time. Lessons or practice? Games or recitals?

I chose soccer, which is Daddy's favorite thing.

Something about that wood thrush singing that lucky song this morning pulls me right out of bed and into my favorite place—the Cave. My closet. A narrow rectangle, just long enough and wide enough to hold my sleeping bag and a pillow. There's a stack of old photographs and a shoebox full of fortunes on one end, and down at the other end, hidden out of sight, is Flicker.

I plop down on my sleeping bag, reach for my flute case, and unlock it as softly as I can. I run my fingers over the shiny silver parts and assemble them. I take a deep breath and activate Quiet Mode before starting the fun part of *The Barber of Seville*. Quiet Mode is when I blow softly across my flute. I can still hear the notes, but nobody else can. It's almost like the wind is blowing, carrying a faint tune.

No one knows I still play my flute. My parents

think I abandoned it the way kids leave behind old toys, but I could never abandon Flicker. It's just that I don't want Daddy to wonder where my heart is. It's with soccer. With him.

So I keep Flicker to myself. Every now and again I slip up and play a few notes out loud, but not this morning. This morning is a soccer morning, and an important one at that. It's the last game of the season, and the Astros are undefeated. We want to keep it that way. No one would understand why I'm suddenly playing my flute instead of doing soccer drills or getting dressed. So I have to be extra careful. Quiet Mode it is.

"MJ! Are you awake?" Daddy's voice startles me. I can tell he's already halfway up the stairs. I shove Flicker into my sleeping bag and jump up to answer.

"I'm awake, Daddy!"

"Just checking! I didn't hear you moving around yet." He knocks and swings open my bedroom door, whisking something in a glass bowl. "Champions need breakfast. I'm making pancakes!"

"That doesn't look like pancake batter!"

"This is the winning marinade. Marinade . . ." He points to me to finish.

"Not sauce!" we say together, and laugh.

He puts his nose right up to the orangey-brown mixture and inhales. "Ooh wee!"

I shake my head. Later today is the big Grill-Off. It's our first cookout of the summer, and it's always a big deal.

"Anything special in your pancakes?"

"Extra chocolate chips, please!"

"You got it. Let's go, Astros!" he yells.

I laugh and hurry to get dressed, but I roll my eyes at my uniform. My name is Maya Jenkins, *MJ* for short, but my uniform says *Maya*. Nobody calls me *Maya* except people who don't know me very well . . . and Mama.

After I'm dressed in our home whites, I pause in the mirror. I practice my game face, the stern look that shows the other team you mean business. But the deep dimples in my brown cheeks erase the sting, and I still look pretty friendly. I shrug and run my hands over my dark brown hair. It's parted down the middle, cornrows on each side like always.

I'm ready. There's only one thing left to do: spin my Wheel of Fortunes. The Wheel is a cardboard circle mounted on my wall. It's cobalt blue, the color of the oceans you see in pictures of Earth from outer space. The outside edges are crammed with pasted-on fortunes from fortune cookies. Every morning (and whenever I need good luck), my favorite thing to do is spin the Wheel until my chopstick points to one thin rectangle of wisdom. Each fortune is a compass, leading me in the right direction.

I close my eyes, concentrate on soccer, and give it a whirl. It lands on:

You have firm convictions—stand strong behind them.

I read it out loud three times to lock it in. Then I kiss Daddy's picture for extra good luck—the one of him as a kid in his royal blue Chargers uniform.

On the way out my room, I steal a look back at the Cave to make sure Flicker is safely out of sight.

CHAPTER 2

Let's Go Play
Some Football!

Your talents will be recognized
and rewarded.

"Let's go play some footballlllll!"

That's Daddy, dragging the *l* for extra drama. He yells this at the beginning of every game, giving it his whole heart and soul. His gleaming bald head thrown back, hands cupped around his mouth, no shame, he takes a deep breath and lets it rip.

Is it embarrassing? Absolutely! But I love it because I love *him*.

Mama says Daddy's a soccer snob, calling it *football* like that. They both grew up right here in Georgia, so they know what the word *football* means to everyone else. But Daddy doesn't care. He fell in love with soccer a million gazillion years ago, back when he was my age.

"It's silly, MJ," he said to me once. "You spend the whole game passing and catching a ball with your *hands*, and Americans have the nerve to call that *football*." He joins in with the rest of the world, calling soccer by its proper name.

Even though he yells "Let's go play some football" at the beginning of every game, we're almost *done* with this one. He's rallying the Astros, because if someone doesn't hurry up and score before time runs out, our last game will end in a tie. Nobody wants a tie. Especially not Daddy and me.

I sneak a look at the clock. Two minutes left. Still enough time to win. I never, ever give up, not until the final whistle blows. *But no one is where they should be.* I sigh.

"Come on!" I shout to anyone who'll listen. *Keep it together, MJ,* I remind myself, blowing out a big puff of air. I get my love of soccer from Daddy, but my firecracker fuse from Mama.

My best friend, Ginger, hustles and as soon as she's in position, we start the dance. She nutmegs the midfielder and runs ahead. It's a slick move, and Daddy shouts, "Ooh wee!" from the sidelines. Then she passes it to me.

We dash from the midfield, adding Angelica to the party, shaking defenders and passing our way to the top. And then I see it, clear as day, the perfect opening for a shot on goal. Wanda's calling for the ball, but I lock eyes with Meisha. I pass it to Ginger to set it up.

"MJ! Wanda is right there!" Angelica shouts, running past, trying to boss me around as usual. *You have firm convictions—stand strong behind them.* I ignore her and pass it to Meisha. The crowd rumbles. This is it! Meisha takes one touch, just one. And boom! She smashes a rocket just past the keeper's fingertips and into the top corner.

A thing of beauty.

We all rush over to Meisha, screaming, dancing, hugging in a huge bunch. I'm the smallest one in the group, but I might be the most excited.

When the whistle blows to end the game, the groan on the other side of the field is drowned out by our parents going wild, cheering, whooping it up. I can't help but wonder if Mama is one of them—if she's smiling, at least.

Mama is not showy. Daddy is a pick-you-up,

swing-you-around, yell-"I love you"-across-the-field type. Mama is a squeeze-your-hand, caress-your-face, and whisper-in-your-ear type. She doesn't use a lot of words or volume to tell you she is worried or happy or mad. She does it in looks and touches and small movements.

One is not better or worse than the other. They are just different.

Though she is stingier with her smiles than Daddy is, she seems to be giving them even less lately. I notice it most at the games or whenever someone brings up soccer. But even outside of soccer, her smiles seem shallow now. They start and stop at her face. When was the last time she smiled a real smile? A deep one. The kind that starts all the way from your toes, rumbles up through your belly, and lights up everything around you.

Weeks? Months? I'm not exactly sure. It's been gradual, like the dimmer switch in our living room. It starts at full brightness, but you can ease the switch down until the darkness is bigger than the light, and shadows take over the whole room. It's cool when you're watching a movie. It's not so cool when you're watching your mom.

After a quick closing huddle and photos with Coach, I run to the sidelines. Daddy and Mama clap and give me matching thumbs-up. I hug and kiss them quick before dashing off with Ginger and Angelica. Win or lose, if it's warm, we get ice cream.

"Congratulations, Babygirl!" shouts Daddy. "Great assist on that goal!"

"I'm proud of you," says Mama. I want to believe her, but even now her smile is barely reaching her eyes.

"Looked like the MVP to me!"

"Mathew . . ." A small warning tone from Mama.

"Whoa!" Daddy throws up his hands in retreat. "I don't vote on these things. I'm just saying, she *looked* like the MVP."

Mama shakes her head at him. The little smile she had is all gone now. I wish I could make her understand. Deep down, I *do* want to be named MVP. If you want to play for a better team, being the season MVP gives you an edge. It'll bring me that much closer to the big goal—becoming a Charger like Daddy was. Our closing banquet is less than a week away, and the MVP will be announced then.

"Have fun, baby," says Mama, planting a loud kiss on my cheek. I can tell she means that, at least.

Just before my friends and I pile into the van, I sneak one more look at my parents. Daddy with his deep brown skin, bald head, and easy smile. Mama, the shortest mom out here, with her spiky fade and cherry-red lips. They are chatting with the other parents, both smiling now. I'm probably the only one who wonders where the *rest* of her smile is.

★ ★ ★

We jump back into Angelica's van, giggling, slurping, and wiping away drips from our waffle cones.

"Try to get the ice cream in your mouth, not on the seats," Mr. Gus says. He looks at me and Ginger through his rearview mirror. "Y'all made some great plays today. Did you have fun?"

"It was fun, but we took it to the wire! Y'all had me stressed," I say.

"Yasss! Today was great, but the whole season was fire," says Ginger. "Even the practices were pretty good."

"This was our best season yet," Angelica says with her mouth full of ice cream. "I can't believe it's almost time for tryouts."

"I know," I say. "Are y'all staying with rec soccer or moving to club?"

"Club definitely. *If* we get picked. You have to be *good* to make a club team," says Angelica.

She's right. Anyone in the neighborhood can sign

up for recreational soccer, and they try to set the teams based on who is just learning and who has the game down pretty well. Then there's club soccer. That's exclusive. You have to be *really* good at soccer to play on a club team. Only the best get chosen. Since there are just a few slots, you really have to dazzle them at tryouts. It helps if you can stand out in some way to the coaches.

"I wanna play for the—"

"Chargers!" Ginger and Angelica beat me to the punch.

"Seems like everybody wants to be a Charger. Except for Meisha," Angelica announces to the van.

"What do you mean?" I ask.

"She's quitting," Angelica fake whispers.

"Whaaaat?" Now it's my turn to shout with Ginger.

Meisha scored the only goal of the whole game. It seems impossible she would stop playing. She's a fantastic striker.

"Why?" I ask.

"She likes soccer, but she doesn't love it. She said she doesn't want to spend all her time at practices and games in middle school."

"I'm sure her parents are happy," says Mr. Gus.

"It's *your* sport, but we have to play it, too. Taking you to practice. Games. Ice cream."

"Dad!" laughs Angelica.

"What's she gonna do instead?" asks Ginger.

Angelica shrugs.

Whatever she wants. That's the seesaw. Soccer on the one end, and whatever else you like to do on the other. *Like more time for flute lessons and playing in a band.* I shake my head to clear the thought away.

"*I'm* not quitting. I *love* soccer. I love every minute!" says Angelica. "You hear that, Daddy? I. Love. Every. Minute."

"Me too," shouts Ginger, holding what's left of her ice cream in a salute.

"Me three."

"Cheers!" We all toast, raising our cones with Ginger.

"Girls! Watch out! No drips!"

"Okay, Daddy, okay!" yells Angelica as Mr. Gus lets me out in front of the house.

"Y'all coming to the Grill-Off later?" I ask everyone.

"Wouldn't miss it!" says Mr. Gus. "I got my money on your father to win again this year."

I wave to their nods and smiles as the van goes three doors down to drop off Ginger next. Back in my room, I decide to do a quick spin of the Wheel before changing for the Grill-Off. I think about today's game, and how Daddy said I looked like an MVP. I hold my breath as the Wheel whirls around, and smile when it lands on: *Your talents will be recognized and rewarded.*

Maybe MVP is in my future after all.

CHAPTER 3

☆

Grill Master

Beauty surrounds you because
you create it.

The strong scent of charcoal and lighter fluid tickles my nose. I smile. Year after year Mama tries to convince Daddy to get a gas grill. "Next year, Leah, maybe next year," he says every time. Then summer rolls around, and he's hauling out a big blue-and-white sack of charcoal briquettes and pouring them into the mouth of the old grill. He drenches the black stones with lighter fluid and tosses in a match. It smells horrible, but I love it. It means music and food and fun, and lots of smack-talking between Daddy and Uncle Jimmy. I spin the Wheel once more and read the fortune out loud: "*Beauty surrounds you because you create it.*" Sounds good to me. I head outside to join the fun.

The first cookout of the year is the big Grill-Off. Uncle J brings his grill and his playlists and his homemade barbecue sauce. This cookout is really a cook-*off* to see who will claim the title of Grill Master. The feature is almost always ribs, but sometimes it's chicken and one year they did lamb. Friends and neighbors drop by and "vote," which means they eat a full plate with offerings from each grill and then claim they can't pick a winner.

"Y'all outdid yourselves!" they say.

"It's just too good, Mat. And you, too, Jimmy. How can I pick? Let me taste another drumstick, and then I can *really* let you know."

Daddy's first love is baking, but he will not be outdone on the grill. He has a whole elaborate routine where he mixes mustard and Worcestershire sauce and stuff like that. He marinates the food in huge containers, setting and resetting timers all day long. And with all the spices and flavors he swirls together, what you won't do is call it barbecue sauce. Absolutely positively no barbecue sauce. We don't buy it. We don't make it. We don't keep any in the house. That's why Uncle Jimmy brings his own.

"If you gotta slather it with all that sauce once you're done cooking, that means you hiding something!" Daddy says.

"Barbecue with no barbecue sauce is just silly, Mathew. Who raised you??"

They go back and forth like this all afternoon, and it cracks me up. Uncle Jimmy knows exactly who raised Daddy. They're identical twins. They both have moles on their faces and dimples in their chins, clean-shaven bald heads, and trimmed mustaches. But Uncle Jimmy has a crisp goatee with sharp lines while Daddy has a full beard. Daddy shaves the beard every summer, so I guess it'll be gone any day now.

"I am planning to show you how it's done with these ribs. Again." Uncle J dramatically snatches away a sheet of heavy-duty foil to unveil a slab ready for the grill. "Look, Baker Man, just leave these to me." He makes a big show of tossing a dash of salt. "I'll handle the tough parts."

"Man, be quiet! You mean, you'll make the parts tough! And why you can't follow directions? I asked you to bring some sweet peppers."

"My bad, you right. I forgot you wanted to do shish kebabs." Uncle J looks at me like no one in their right mind would ever make such a thing at a cook-off, and could I believe it? I giggle, looking to see what Daddy's gonna say next. He smacks Uncle Jimmy in the chest.

"Watch out, now! Don't hurt yourself!" teases Uncle J, flexing his muscles.

We all erupt into big laughs as Uncle J spots Mama walking toward us loaded down with plates and napkins.

"How's my favorite sister doing?" he says, cozying up to her and freeing her hands.

"It's good to see you, Jimmy," says Mama. She sounds happy, but one quick look and I see she's smiling only halfway. She's usually as excited as everyone else for the Grill-Off. Ready to outdance the newbies while the folks who know better eat seconds and thirds of her potato salad instead. Although Mama is not one for being loud or showy most of the time, dancing is her big joy.

It's not my imagination. Her light is definitely dimmer.

After the first sizzles on the grill, Uncle J calls out to me, "You hanging with me this summer, or are you getting too old for that?"

"I'm hanging!"

He's a music teacher at the high school, and there's live music in the park all summer long. Mostly we just go and lie in the sun and listen to the bands. Sometimes his students perform, and once in a while he even jams with them. I've never played, of course, but a long time ago I wanted to.

Maybe, deep down, I still do.

"I'm just glad you still have time for me. I heard I missed your big assist, superstar!"

"That's my babygirl right there!" shouts Daddy. "Soon-to-be Astros MVP and a future Charger!"

Mama cuts her eyes sharp and quick at Daddy then, dropping the temperature of the whole outside by twenty degrees with just one look.

"Whew, it got frosty out here," says Uncle J, trying to lighten the mood. "Let me go check on my grill and make sure it's still working!" Although he turns away, I'm pretty sure he's still listening.

"We talked about this, Mat."

I can't see her face, but I can tell from her tone that her eyebrows are up in the *You're getting told off* position.

"I'm just having fun, Leah." Daddy leans in and lowers his voice, but I can hear him ask, "Can't we just do this?" I'm guessing "this" is the cookout, but I'm not so sure.

Mama storms toward the house without so much as a glance in my direction. Daddy winks at me like it's no big deal, but I've heard them whisper-fighting more than once the past couple of months. At first, I thought it was just a soccer thing. Every time Daddy mentions the Chargers, she gets mad and calls him obsessed. But deep down, I know it's more than that.

Beauty surrounds you because you create it. I'm not sure how I can create beauty from this.

⭐

CHAPTER 4

Before I Let Go

You will find your solution where
you least expect it.

I go to the kitchen in search of Daddy's extra marinade. Mama is stirring her famous potato salad.
Only she's not really stirring it, she's pounding it,
slamming a wooden spoon into the glass bowl over
and over again. Her face is one big scowl. I'm afraid
to interrupt, but I don't see the mason jar.

"Have you seen Daddy's marinade?"

She slaps her chest. "You startled me."

"Sorry."

She points wordlessly to the jar on the table, which
is almost hidden between serving dishes.

"It's fine. Where's Ginger?" she asks, still stirring but no longer slamming into the bowl.

"She's on the way. Everybody's coming."

"Good." She pauses. "Maya?"

"Yes, Mama?"

She looks at me. Her face is soft, like she wasn't just upset a few seconds ago. That's something else we have in common. Quick to anger, but usually quick to cool, too. I wonder if she will say something like *Don't worry about me and Daddy* or *Good luck with MVP at the banquet next week. I know how much it means to you.* But she doesn't say any of that. She doesn't say anything at all.

"Never mind." She covers the potato salad and puts it in the fridge. I watch her to see if she will change her mind again, but she takes her time at the fridge and I finally give up.

After I deliver Daddy's marinade, I hide out in my Cave and sort through old fortunes. I wish I knew how to cheer Mama up. How to make her smile a real smile again. *You will find your solution where you least expect it,* says one of the fortunes in my stack. I try to imagine the unexpected, but nothing comes to mind.

I don't know about helping Mama, but I do know Flicker will cheer *me* up at least. *The Barber of Seville* will do the trick, although I'm still getting the hang of it, and I have to take my time when I play.

Even in my closet on Quiet Mode, playing Flicker sweeps me away to some other place. A bright place where the sun is always shining and I feel love or beauty or hope—all the good things that make me feel powerful inside. Playing Flicker cheers me up when I'm sad, and it makes me triple cheerful if I'm already in a good mood. I can play slow songs or fight songs or anthems, or the fun notes of cartoons, and even though I haven't mastered all of that yet, it's still the best feeling in the world.

Just as the laughter and music outside let me know the Grill-Off is getting into full swing, my door flies open. Ginger drops into a fighting stance, belting out a joyful "Hey!" I shove my flute out of sight and hurry out of the Cave. Even though she's my best friend, I haven't told her about my playing, either. I feel funny about that, but I just don't want anyone else to know.

"You made it!"

"I made it!" she sings back, shimmying into my room. "I can't stay the whole time, though."

"Whaddya mean?"

"Pa Pa's coming over."

"So? He can just come with your parents."

"They're not coming, either. We're going . . . somewhere else." I frown, surprised, and questions bubble up inside me. I want to ask her where *somewhere else* is. But at the same time, why would I have to ask? We tell each other everything. At least I thought we did. And did I imagine it, or did her face twitch when she said *somewhere else*? Like maybe she feels guilty about not saying where. But she breezes on, so maybe I'm overreacting.

"They want pictures and plates, though. They said they have to vote on Grill Master."

"Whatever! You have to be here to vote." I toss a pillow at her. We break into giggles and plop down on the floor.

Her parents have never missed a Grill-Off, but I'm sort of relieved they're not coming. That means no soccer talk between her dad and mine. Maybe Mama will even relax and dance.

"Angelica said she'll be here in a second."

"You talked to her since ice cream?"

"Yeah, just for a minute." My stomach drops. I don't remember Ginger and Angelica ever hanging out without me. It's always been the two of us—*sometimes* the three of us, but never just the two of them. She breezes on again.

"Chaos is coming, too! He has a big announcement," she says, using a grown-up announcer voice.

"Oh yeah? What is it?"

"I don't know." She shrugs.

We're quiet for a while, imagining his big news.

"Thumb wars, let's go!" she shouts, and throws out a thumb to wrestle. We lock fingers and yell out together, "I. De. Clare. War!" We shriek and wiggle until I win.

"Again!" she yells. More twisting and screaming, and she takes the win this time. We lay back, dissolving into giggles as the opening notes of Frankie Beverly and Maze's "Before I Let Go" float up from the backyard.

"Uncle J is playing the wrong version!" I shout from the floor.

"Where's Beyoncé when you need her?" Ginger asks the ceiling in fake despair. We laugh again.

"Let's go show them how it's done," I say, jumping up. Ginger hops up laughing, grabs my hand, and leads the way out.

Chaos and Angelica are already sipping punch by the time we get outside.

"Ahh, there you are," Chaos says as we approach.

"What's that?" I ask, pointing at what might be a necklace, except it looks like an oversize smile across his neck. The bright white teeth stand out against his deep brown skin, and I don't think I've ever seen him wear jewelry before. "Are those . . . teeth?"

Angelica grimaces and shakes her head, like she doesn't wanna know. But I do.

"Teeth, yes! It's National Smile Day. And you know what they say"—he points to his necklace—"you're never fully dressed without a smile."

We all groan and laugh as we fix our plates and sit down facing each other on the grass.

"Spill the beans, Chaos," says Angelica.

"Yeah, what's the news?" Ginger asks.

He clears his throat and pauses, looking at each of us to make sure we're listening.

"The new pool is finally opening."

We all clap. Even Chaos cheers at his own announcement. The pool has been closed all year for a huge makeover, and we weren't sure when it would reopen. Ginger is probably the most excited of everyone, though. She's a water baby. She learned to swim before she could talk.

That makes one of us. As much as we played in

the pool every year, I never learned to swim. Not very well, anyway. Our neighborhood pool wasn't that deep, so it didn't matter much.

"When is the grand opening?" I ask.

"Next weekend! After the last day of school. It's going to be quite different now."

"Bigger, right?" asks Angelica.

"Twice the size." Chaos nods, throwing up two fingers on both hands. "And they've added a water slide, too. There will also be new rules since the pool is so big."

"New rules? Like what?" I ask.

"Unfortunately," says Chaos, "those details were not revealed. But I'm sure we will come to know them very soon."

"Well, whatever the rules are, we'll all be there, and we'll all have fun together," declares Ginger. With that, she holds up her cup of punch and the rest of us do, too. We all say "cheese" in honor of National Smile Day and "cheers" to a great summer ahead.

CHAPTER 5

⭐

Cloudy

Do not dwell on differences with a
loved one. Try to compromise.

At the beginning of PE, everyone sits on the
bleachers waiting for Mr. Lew to take attendance
and tell us today's agenda. But I spend those first five
minutes on my soccer drills. I have a whole routine:
sole rolls, L drags, inside outs, and other stuff. All
together it's 500 touches.

Daddy says doing these drills is one of the secrets
to getting great with the ball, but I like doing them. I
love the feeling of mastering things. I've been doing
them all year, and even though the season is techni-
cally over, I don't wanna stop. At least not until I bring

home the Golden Astro. That's our MVP award, and the winner gets announced at the banquet tonight.

Ginger usually does them with me. But for some reason she hasn't moved yet. She's sitting there on the bleachers, talking to Angelica. I don't know why they're spending more time together lately. Angelica is okay, but she's not my favorite person. She's always telling me what else I could've done instead of whatever I chose to do. Like at the game when she yelled at me for not passing to Wanda.

I set the ball down on the floor between my feet. I steal another look, hoping Ginger's on the way. She isn't even looking in my direction. Something's off. In fact, the whole gym seems cloudy today. I didn't know it was possible for a room to seem cloudy if Ginger was in it.

Ginger has bright red hair. Well, they call it red, but I think it's closer to orange. The same color as the sunset when it's going to be hot the next day. A fiery, orange red stealing your attention whenever she walks into a room. Or poses, because she's always doing some kind of ninja stance. Which is really funny since she doesn't like to argue or fight. Ginger is a peace-maker.

Her face is full of freckles covering her light brown

skin, and they're the same fiery, orange red as her hair. In the middle of it all is her huge smile. When she's happy, you can see all of her teeth, like one of those old jazz singers, mouth open wide, joy bursting. And she's always smiling. Ginger is the sun brightening everything. She's the one I share Deep Downs with. That's what we call our heavy thoughts and feelings—the stuff we're too embarrassed or scared to tell anyone else.

With Ginger, everything is better.

I fight the urge to call her over and start my touches instead. Inside outside with the right foot first. Fifty repetitions, and then I switch to the left. I slip into a rhythm while daydreaming about tonight's soccer banquet. If all goes according to plan, I'll be that much closer to becoming a Charger.

"Hey!"

I nearly trip at the sound of Ginger's voice, but I stop the ball before it rolls away. I look up and see Angelica, tall and slim with a fluffy twist out on top, standing right behind Ginger. Hovering. A bodyguard.

"Coming?" Ginger asks.

Without even thinking, I reach out my hand to hers. She reaches back. Whenever Ginger invites me anywhere, she grabs my hand and pulls me with her.

Like my yes is implied in her invitation. And it is. Always. She squeezes my hand, but she doesn't really . smile. Then she lets it go.

"What's wrong?" I mouth to her. She shakes her head. Even though I know better, I let it go for now.

"Where?" I ask.

"Three v three. Now." Angelica butts in, hand on her hip, with a face that says hurry up.

"But—"

"We're not doing it last today." Angelica cuts me off. "Mr. Lew gave us free period since it's the last week of school. You in or what?"

I know it's silly, but besides the fun of mastering the drills, I don't want to do anything to jinx my chances for the MVP tonight. It's like a good-luck charm. Some people will always eat the same dinner before a big game. Other people will always wear the same shirt or socks. I want to do the same drills. Mama thinks it's superstitious, but Daddy understands. Plus, the drills are good for alone time with Ginger, and I could use that now. To see what's wrong. To see why she seems so cloudy today.

"Hello? Earth to MJ," blurts Angelica. "Can't you skip the touches today? The season is over."

"Three minutes. I'm almost done." I feel my

temperature rising, but I swallow it down and restart my touches. I'm on the inside-out V cuts now.

Angelica rolls her eyes. "Forget it. Wanda's ready." She turns and waves across the gym.

A ray of sunshine cuts through the clouds as Ginger reaches for my hand again. I stop the ball and squeeze her.

"Still doing touches?" she asks me just above a whisper.

"Yeah."

"Getting ready for club team tryouts already?"

I nod, even though it's only partly true.

"Are you gonna be obsessed with the Chargers forever?"

"No. Yes." We crack up laughing.

"Ginger!" Angelica shouts.

"Wait." I pull her closer. "Tell me what's wrong, first."

The clouds return. "Later. Promise. Hurry and finish! I'll sub you in. I'll see you at the banquet."

She turns and jogs away. I stare after her. She'll *see* me there? We always go together. Now I *really* wonder what's up.

I have 150 touches left, but I start over. Again.

Cloudy. Definitely cloudy.

CHAPTER 6

☆

Maybe. Maybe Not.

You may lose the small ones but
win the big ones.

T-minus two hours and counting until the closing
banquet—my last one as an Astro. Nothing would
make Daddy and me happier than bringing home that
Golden Astro MVP trophy.

I already know exactly where it would go: the living room Wall of Fame. It started off as a bookcase,
but we cleared off some of the shelves and filled them
with Daddy's soccer trophies instead. When I got my
first one, a small, lightweight statue of a girl kicking
a ball, he cleared off another shelf and put my trophy
right in the middle. Now I have seven trophies just

like that first one. If I get the Golden Astro, it will take center stage.

When I get to Daddy's office, he waves me in, but his lips are tight. He's upset about something. Voices erupt from his speaker. He turns down the volume and mutes his phone.

"There's my MJ!" He tries to sound cheerful, but it's hard to pull off with tight lips. "School was okay?"

"Yeah. It's the last week, so nothing much is going on."

He nods. "Got a question for ya. What do you call a dad when he falls through the ice?"

"I give."

"A Popsicle!"

"Daddy," I groan.

"I know, I know." He pauses and rubs his hand over his head. "I've got some bad news, Babygirl." My stomach flutters as he strides over to me. He never has bad news. "I have to miss the banquet."

"Daddy!"

His lips are still tight, but my stomach is tighter. I can't believe it. Daddy and I always go together. Always. After every banquet, we even do a whole routine. He smiles and asks: "Are you in for next season?"

And every time, I answer with his cheer: "Yes! Let's go play some footballlllll!" And we laugh on the way home. Every time, like clockwork.

"Mama's going this time," he says. I frown at this news. It's just hard to imagine. The banquets are *our* thing. And it's not just any banquet, it's *the* banquet. The big one.

"Why can't you go?"

He pauses at first, like he's looking for the missing words. "I have a couple of meetings tonight, and she's never taken you. We thought it would be fun to switch it up."

They thought it would be "fun" to switch it up? Mama doesn't even like soccer all that much. How could that be fun?

"It's okay," I say quietly, without meeting his eyes. It's not okay, though. He's never missed a banquet, and I've never had a chance to get a real trophy. Now both things are happening at the same time.

"I'm sorry," he says, hugging me while the work voices continue swirling in the background. I know he means it, but it doesn't take the sting away.

"You know I definitely want to go, right? I'm missing out on the pizza."

I smile a little at that. Banquet pizza is okay, but it's not Daddy's. He can make anything, even pizza, from scratch.

"Here." He pulls a wrinkled rectangle from his pocket and hands it to me. It's a fortune. *You may lose the small ones but win the big ones.* "*Tonight* is a big one," he whispers, smiling. "Take pictures so you can tell me all about it."

I nod.

"I'm sorry, Babygirl." He rubs my nose with his and heads back to his desk. "You and Mama will have a good time."

Maybe. Maybe she'll see how much soccer means to me. Maybe she will smile a real smile. Maybe.

CHAPTER 7

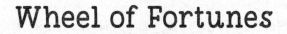

Wheel of Fortunes

All the preparation you've done
will finally be paying off!

I mope all the way to my room. I can't believe Daddy won't be there. He's *always* there, holding my hand or doing funny cheers when everyone wins awards. We eat the pizza pretending to be food critics talking about the generous slices, with the sparse toppings, on gooey crust. Ginger usually joins in the fun, but . . .

"I'll see you there." That's what she'd said. She's never "seen me there." We always go there—we always go *everywhere*—together. That's what best friends do. I wonder what she wants to tell me.

I grab a bottle of rubber cement to add Daddy's

fortune to the Wheel. Mama and I made it back when I was in second grade. By then, we'd finally figured out the best way to eat fortune cookies: first. Before the vegetable lo mein and shrimp fried rice, everyone grabs a cookie. You crack it in half and pull out the slip of paper, but you don't read it yet. Not until you crunch and munch that crispy wafer to nothing. You wash it all down and clear your throat. Then, and only then, you read your fortune out loud to everyone else.

I remember the night the Wheel was born. Things started as they always did. Mama cleared her throat and read her fortune: "*You deserve to have a good time after a hard day's work.* Can I get an amen?" she asked.

"Amen!" shouted Daddy and me.

"That's right," she said, "this queen is taking it easy this weekend. Who's next?"

"Me," boomed Daddy. He cleared his throat and smoothed out the narrow strip. "*A leader is powerful to the degree he empowers others.* Exactly. I'm large and in charge!" He flexed a bicep. I thumped it.

"It doesn't say large or in charge!"

"It says the queen deserves to take it easy, so as the powerful leader, I'm empowering the princess to do some chores."

"Daddy!"

"Great idea, Mat."

"My turn." I cleared my throat and read mine, the weirdest fortune of all. *"You have the power to write your own fortune."*

"Ooooohhh." Mama and Daddy both sounded impressed. I wasn't.

"It's telling you to make things happen, fiya-cracker," Mama explained. "It's your world! That's a good one. You should keep it."

"I'm keeping them all," I announced, and put them in a little pile at my elbow as we finally started to eat. That's when it happened—when Mama gave me the idea to make the Wheel of Fortunes.

That weekend, I gathered all the fortunes I could find around the house. It's not like we ever really threw them away. We ordered Chinese takeout every Friday, so you could always find a few fortunes here or there. On the fridge, in drawers. Together we cut out and painted the cardboard circle and stuck all the little slips of paper on the wheel, starting with the one she liked so much: *You have the power to write your own fortune.*

"Never forget that, Maya, my fiya-cracker," she said, rubbing my cheek. Ever since then, I spin it every day. Sometimes more than once. Every now and then,

I add new ones or take old ones off. Like now.

"Maya? Are you getting ready?" Mama's voice cuts through my thoughts. I hadn't heard her come home.

"Yes, ma'am."

She opens the door all the way. She's still dressed up from work: dark cherry lipstick as usual, with her sparkling nose ring, plus a choker necklace, the kind that wraps around her whole neck. She's always sharp!

"This is you getting ready?" she laughs. "It looks like you're just standing at the Wheel." Her face is soft now. Not the sharp look she has whenever Daddy is joking about soccer. I am still sad he's not going, but maybe he's right. Maybe we really will have a good time.

"I'm getting ready."

"Are you riding with Ginger, or is Ginger riding with us?"

I shrug.

"Something happen between you two?"

"No. . . . She said she'd see me there."

"Oh. Well." Mama pauses, looking around the room. She doesn't mention the board games and soccer gear strewn on the floor, and Flicker is still out of sight. "Let's skedaddle. You don't want to be late."

When she leaves, I concentrate on the banquet,

give the Wheel a good spin, and cover my eyes, waiting for it to stop. I peek through my fingers to read the verdict:

All the preparation you've done will finally be paying off!

I hope so.

Maybe by the time I get back home, I'll know what's up with Ginger, I'll have a new trophy to show Daddy, and I'll be a huge step closer to becoming a Charger. I kiss the picture of Daddy the Charger for extra good luck. Then I get dressed in my bright yellow shirt and prepare for the best.

CHAPTER 8

The Golden Astro

You will soon be receiving some
wonderful news.

Mama and I make it to the banquet hall just in time. Everyone else is seated at round tables covered in black or yellow tablecloths, topped with sparkly confetti. Just seeing the team colors and the trophies lined up across the front brings a huge smile to my face. It's all I can do not to run up front and take a closer look.

I scan the room for Ginger. I shake my head when I see I can't sit beside her as I'd planned. Her dad is on the one side and her grandfather, Pa Pa, is on the other. Pa Pa is a charmer. When he talks to you, you feel welcome, as if you're in just the right place at just the right time. He's always smiling with his sparkly white teeth and white hair to match, while telling long stories that have you holding your side, laughing by the end. We all wave hello as Mama and I join them. Ginger shrugs as I sit down. I shrug back. I guess her news will have to wait.

We chomp our not-so-delicious pizza, and someone starts the season-in-review video. This time they set it to "Uptown Funk" by Bruno Mars. All the heads are nodding, and some folks are dancing in their seats. Even Mama is clapping along, shaking her shoulders and laughing.

I giggle watching her. There's the dancer I remember. She loves all dance, but she's a salsera, a salsa dancer, at heart. She used to dance anytime we turned on the Afro Cuban Jazz station. She even taught me how to do shines, the fancy footwork that dancers do to show off. I'm surprised she's having so much fun at a soccer event, but I'm glad.

We all whoop and clap at the snapshots of our undefeated record and the final game. All of us are midscream, cheering. Ginger and I are hugging, smiling so huge, our faces disappear. She turns around and winks at me, like everything is fine. Maybe I've just been too nervous about the banquet. Maybe everything really *is* fine. I wink back.

Coach taps the mic to announce the special trophies. He starts with the Sensational Spirit Award, telling us how important it is to have a good attitude and be cheerful no matter what. He goes on like that for a while, and then he reveals the winner: Queenie Williams. We laugh and clap because who else could it be?

He makes his way through the next few trophies— Lightning Striker, Distinguished Defender, Hotfoot Hustler—when finally, the time is here. When he says "Golden Astro," I sit up straight and clasp my fingers together, like saying grace. I look at Mama, to see if she understands what a big deal this is. She smiles at me, but she doesn't give any sign that she knows this is critical. I inhale all the way to my toes and wait. All eyes are on Coach.

"This award," he explains, "goes to the best all-around player. If she's not on the field, you're worried, but if she's there, you know you've still got a chance. She's a natural leader on and off the field. She's optimistic and even-tempered. A calming force. She's spontaneous, able to improvise even under pressure." My hands shake.

Coach gets louder. Preaching, really, about this award. I'm expecting someone to yell "Amen!" Everyone leans forward, awaiting the news. I see lightning bolts from the Chargers' uniform flashing in my mind.

"This award represents the best of who we are." I squeeze my hands even tighter. *All the preparation you've done will finally be paying off!* Let it be me, *please.* Please let me receive some wonderful news.

"Put your hands together for this year's best of the best. Our Golden Astro, Ms. Georgianna 'Ginger' Scott!"

I gasp, stuck to my chair, as the whole team stands as one and whoops. Like they knew she deserved it the whole time. Like she was the obvious choice.

Mama elbows me, her cherry lips stern. Ginger turns and looks at me, sunshiny smile and all. And even though I hurry to smile at her, I know it's too late. She sees my shock and dismay. *He picked her?* It's written all over my face. More than that, it's written all over my heart. She blushes as I finally stand up and clap along with everyone else, hoping with everything in me that no tears will rain down.

Mama elbows me again as she smiles and claps toward Ginger's dad. He nods to the table, clapping proud, just like my daddy would if he were here and it were me.

Ginger skips to the front to get her trophy. Even as I watch her accept the award, I still hope there was a mistake. That maybe the base has my name engraved on it, or maybe both of ours.

"Fix your face, Maya." Mama elbows me so hard this time, I think I will get a frog in my shoulder. Ginger heads back to the table, all smiles still. Teammates give high fives and thumbs-up as she passes them. She and Angelica bump elbows and laugh.

"Maya," Mama whispers in my ear as Ginger gets closer, award held high over her head. "She's your best friend." I nod, but I am still fighting tears.

Ginger flashes us the trophy, and everyone else looks so happy and proud. It's not a mistake. Right there, engraved at the bottom, is her name. Her full name, Georgianna Scott, Golden Astro. It's beautiful—a crystal soccer ball. Makes me feel ugly for being jealous. I want to be happy for her, but I really, really had my heart set on that trophy. The only person in the world who would understand isn't even here.

"Congratulations, Ginger," I say across the table as soon as we all sit down again. "That's really cool!"

I smile as big as I can. Which is pretty small in the grand scheme of things. Shallow. Deep down, I am devastated and embarrassed.

"Thanks, Maya." She smiles back, big as always, but I can tell that she can tell that mine is fake. I want to hug her. To grab her hand. To be best friends anyway. But all I can do is stare at the glass ball. Then I follow the leader as we each pick up our no-name team trophies and listen to Coach tell us all thanks for a great season, and goodbye.

Goodbye, Astros, and goodbye to my best chance at becoming a Charger. My only hope now is soccer camp.

CHAPTER 9

⭐

Bang! Bang!

The greatest achievement in life is
to stand up again after falling.

I am a zombie following Mama out to the car. I hope
no one waves or smiles or says goodbye, because I
don't think I can respond. I am too heartbroken to be
polite.

Of course it was possible I wouldn't get the Golden
Astro, but I never really let myself think about it. Not
after Daddy and I worked so hard. We studied professional games. We studied videos of my games. I did
my touches every single day. I gave every spare minute
to soccer.

"Don't be mad at Ginger," says Mama, observing me with her eagle eye.

"I'm not mad at Ginger."

"You need to fix things with her, Maya," she says, starting the car and backing out.

"Nothing's broken."

"I'm sure she saw the look on your face. Her feelings are probably hurt."

I squeeze my hands. Maybe if I squeeze them hard enough, I won't lose my temper. I'm the one with hurt feelings. No one on the team wanted it as much as me. I remember Daddy's eyes, the way he rubbed his hands when he said he wanted to hear how it went. *Take pictures so you can tell me all about it*, he'd said. I did not take any pictures of Ginger's trophy.

"I know it's hard when your heart is set on something," Mama says, her voice softening as she lets down the windows. "I've been disappointed, too, kiddo. I get it."

I shake my head. I don't wanna talk about it. Especially not with the person who has never loved soccer to begin with. We drive in silence for a while.

"Maya?"

Something about the way she calls my name is

familiar. She pauses without saying anything else, and then I remember that's the same thing she did in the kitchen during the cookout.

"Why don't you try something new this summer? Like go to a sleepaway camp?" She speeds up like she knows she has to hurry and say what's on her mind before we both figure out it's a bad idea.

"There's a cool leadership camp for young artists. Remember when you used to play the flute?"

I wince, nervous that she's discovered my secret flute playing, but if she notices my reaction, she doesn't show it. On she races with her commercial. "They have band, and they have dance, too. It's not too late to sign up."

She pulls a brochure from the center console and hands it to me. Kids fill the cover, some wearing leotards and bright smiles beneath heavy makeup. Others hold a random assortment of instruments. I spot one girl holding a flute and smiling, her mouth full of braces. I catch myself before I smile back at the girl. This could be me posing, except for the braces. I smile this way almost every time I hold Flicker. But I can't be at two camps at the same time.

I lay the brochure facedown in my lap, pretending not to care. Mama keeps going. "The dancers and the band perform together at the end. It looks like fun!"

The exclamation point, the *bang* as Daddy calls it, jumps out of her mouth and fills up the car. Mama is not the kind of person who speaks in bangs. Even when she has good news or is having a good time, there's no exclamation point at the end of her sentences. I frown, suspicious. Why is she bringing up my flute out of the blue anyway? Why is she trying to get me out of soccer?

"I'm going to the soccer ID camp." I don't really have a choice now. Unlike regular summer camps, recruiters and scouts come to the ID camps, to see if you're good enough for their clubs.

"Look at me, Maya," she says at the stoplight. She reaches out to touch my cheek, and the bangles on her wrist jangle in the silence. I meet her eyes, but fight with myself to stay put. I want nothing more than to pull away.

"You're too young to be stuck doing something you don't really love."

"But I do love soccer." *And Daddy loves soccer. You're the only one who doesn't love it*, I think.

"Maybe you do, but there's probably something wrong if you can't be happy to see your best friend win that trophy." That last part feels like fingers jabbing me in my chest. I'm not unhappy that she won. I'm sad I lost. Sad and scared I might not be a Charger after all.

I lean away from her warm touch, scooting as far to my side as possible. She sighs and the light turns green.

"Well, just think about it."

I shake my head and stare out the window, wishing we were already home. Then I ball my hands into tight fists, remembering that once I get there, I'll have nothing to show Daddy. Nothing but nameless trophy number eight.

Daddy's gone when we get back. I hide out in the Cave with my tablet, debating whether to video-call Ginger. Mama's right that I wasn't super nice about her winning. I hope she understands.

I decide to visit the Flute Girl Rocks channel instead. I grab Flicker to play along to some of her old videos. This time it's the scales. Some people might get bored playing scales, but I think they're fun. Plus, I like the easy way the notes step up, peak, and then come down, blending into each other. I don't have to think or feel disappointed. I can just listen to the wind.

After a while, I hear Daddy's voice creeping in under my door. I imagine him asking Mama about the banquet. Her telling him I had to fix my face when Ginger won. That I was not happy for my best friend.

I trudge out of my room to break the news myself, but as I get to the stairs, I can tell a fog has settled in down below. The air is thick and tense, and my ears are filled with the sounds of sharp whispers. Mama's and Daddy's voices are scissors slicing through the heaviness.

They're at it again.

Even in the whispering, I hear Mama giving another exclamation point. Two in one day. This time it's not a happy bang. It's a testy one. "Space!" is all I can make out.

Other words fly up to my ears. "Past time." "Trapped." Are they arguing about soccer? Is she trying to make me quit? Then it sounds as if she's saying something about Daddy leaving. "Maybe it's best . . . ," she says. I grip the banister, waiting for him to respond before I creep farther down the stairs. The silence lasts forever.

When he finally says something, it's so quiet, I can't make out what it is. I can only hear a rumbling thunder. Whatever is going on, it doesn't seem like the time to talk about trophies or soccer or disappointment. *Maybe tomorrow,* I think, and I tiptoe away from the stairs and back into my room.

This day has been the worst. I spin the Wheel, hoping for something good. *The greatest achievement in life is to stand up again after falling.*

I guess so. Surely tomorrow has to be better.

CHAPTER 10

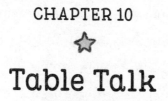

Table Talk

**All things are difficult before they
are easy.**

I'm back home after the last day of school, so it's a
perfect time to celebrate with a march. I pull out
the sheet music for "In Storm and Sunshine" and
start to play on Quiet Mode. I love this march because
the flutes really shine. Some parts remind me of cartoons where wind is whipping all around—I think the
flutes are the wind. Even though it's supposed to be a
storm, it sounds kinda fun.

As wonderful as it is to play it alone, I know it
would be even better with a live band—not just the
videos I watch sometimes. All that music inside you

and surrounding you at the same time? The other woodwinds, plus percussion and brass, too? I tingle just thinking of it. Maybe next summer I'll try that band camp.

"MJ?"

Daddy's voice sounds strange. Strained—almost hoarse—and I am afraid to find out why. It's Fried Rice Friday. That means Mama orders Chinese and we all play board games. But this doesn't sound like game time or fun at all. Before I go down, I spin the Wheel for good luck, although it hasn't worked that well lately. I sigh when I see where it lands: *All things are difficult before they are easy.*

I steal down the stairs as if going quietly will hide me from whatever Daddy wants to say. Our kitchen table is a dark rectangle surrounded by four red chairs. Mama and Daddy sit at the far ends, and they both look at me when I enter the room. Something's definitely up.

"Come sit with us," says Mama. She tries to make it sound casual, but we've never all sat around an empty table. There's always food or games or something. It's never just . . . bare.

"We want to talk to you about this summer."

They've been whispering about something for

days. Whatever it is, it can't be good. I try not to feel angry in advance, but it's too late. The heat is already rising in my chest.

"Is this about band camp?" I ask, but deep down, I know better.

"Did you change your mind about it?" Mama asks. "Do you want to go?"

There it is again. That weird excitement in her voice. It's nervous excitement. Like she hopes I'll say yes.

"I want to play soccer, Mama," I say, keeping my voice even.

"It's not about camp, MJ," Daddy says. His crisp tone and tight lips let me know that the table is empty to make room for a big conversation; serious words that do not sound like a good meal or a fun time. I wait, heart thumping in my throat. Finally, Daddy begins.

"You know how at work, I manage projects?" he asks. "Most of the time they run smoothly, but sometimes there's a problem that's so big, the whole thing is in jeopardy."

I frown, confused. Why is he bringing up work now? Out the corner of my eye, I see Mama shift around in her seat. Her hands are gripped together. Locked, like she's afraid to let one or the other go. The same way I gripped my hands while waiting for Coach to announce the Golden Astro. I've never seen her this way. The butterflies in my stomach take flight.

He sighs. "Sometimes things, important things, don't work out the way you planned. Your mother and I love each other and love you very much."

I open my eyes wide, looking to see where this is going because it can't be heading in the right direction. He grabs my hand. I want to change the grip, to make him thumb wrestle. To interrupt everything and yell:

I. De. Clare. War!

Instead he bulldozes my thoughts and announces, "I'm moving out, Maya. For the summer anyway."

"What?" I snatch my hand away.

"Your father and I are separating," Mama says quietly.

"You're getting a divorce?" I shout.

They lock eyes as if to decide who will respond. I look back and forth between the two of them.

"No," Mama answers first.

"No," Daddy agrees.

"We're separating for *now,*" Mama explains, stressing the *now.* "So we can have some time to think about . . . things."

"Just a few weeks," Daddy says. "Eight, to be exact."

"No!" I shout in shock. "You can't just leave, Daddy. You live here! With me! Where will you go?"

"I have a place. It's very close to here."

"When?" I demand, although I don't really want an answer. When they are both quiet, I fear the worst.

"Tonight?"

"Tomorrow."

I slump in my chair. That's no better.

Mama shifts again and my brain connects the dots. "Wait. Is this why you wanted to send me to band camp? So you guys could break up while I was gone?"

She looks away without denying it. I know I'm right. They wanted to disappear me for their divorce!

"Is this real?"

"Calm down, Maya," she says.

"What did I do?" I ask with less calm and more volume.

"This isn't punishment." The sharp edges in her voice tell me her temper is slipping away along with mine.

"It's just for a little while," says Daddy. "Just for the summer. Eight weeks." He says the last part so quietly, I don't believe it. He doesn't sound anything like the soccer dad who always cheers at the top of his lungs.

He grabs my hand again and I stare at him. Daddy's face, normally so smooth, looks like a puzzle, with sadness etching lines this way and that. I don't want to see him this way. I don't want to see Mama avoiding my questioning eyes.

"I can't believe it. On top of everything, now this?"

At that, Mama finally looks at me. I watch as all the air leaves her chest in one big push. "We love you, Maya. I know you must have questions."

I shake my head. I don't have questions because I don't want answers. I just want them to figure it out. I want my life to be more like my fortunes (the happy ones, at least). I want to receive wonderful news. I want my preparation to pay off. I deserve to have a good time. . . . Instead, I'm stuck on all things being difficult.

I look at the empty table—the place where we play games and eat Daddy's cakes and Chinese takeout—and wonder if I can ever sit there or even look at it again.

I run out of the kitchen and upstairs, away from my parents.

Away from that empty table.

Away.

CHAPTER 11

☆

Get a Clue

In dreams and in life, nothing is
impossible.

"It's not fair!" I yell from the middle of my room.
"It's my life, too!"

Why do parents get to mess up everything? What
if I came in and made a big announcement? "I'm leaving for two months!" They would freak out.

Daddy is always here and now he'll just be *poof*,
gone. I don't care if it's a month or just a week—any
time is too long. And what if they never get back
together? What if it's just me and Mama and her dim-
ming smiles and her scowls at soccer?

I fold my arms super tight across my body, but

what I really wanna do is throw something. A book, a box, something heavy and loud. Instead, I slump over to the Cave and plop down on the floor. I pick up the small stack of old photos from the corner. The top one is Daddy's team photo from when he was a Charger. Two rows of boys in royal blue, but he's the only one with a huge grin. No "game face" for Daddy. All smiles for soccer, even back then.

The next photo is him, too. Standing in front of his grill, he's posing like Superman. Legs spread, fists on his hips, his apron says:

Today's Menu Has Two Choices:
Take It or Leave It!

"Leave it. Definitely."

Eventually I get up and drag myself to the Wheel. *Stay, stay, stay, Daddy. Please stay.* I spin, spin, and release, and close my eyes tight until it's done.

In dreams and in life, nothing is impossible.

That's when it hits me. It's still Friday and there's still time. It's a long shot, but maybe something fun can help turn things around. Last week was Bananagrams, so this week's game letter is *C.* I scan all the

C boxes in my room: Charades, Candy Land, Checkers, Chess. There's also Connect 4 somewhere. But then I see Clue. Boom! It's one of Mama's favorite games, and you must have at least three people to play. I snatch the box from the floor and march to the kitchen like nothing has changed.

The air is thick with tension. But Daddy, still sitting at the table, spots the box and throws me a quick wink. Mama eyes me, then Clue, but she doesn't say anything. Instead, she sighs and turns on the Afro Cuban Jazz station. "Me Gusta Boogaloo" fills the room, and Daddy chuckles, setting up the game.

Mama orders Chinese. "Yes, we'll have the usual, please." That's vegetable lo mein, shrimp fried rice with extra shrimp, and chicken with broccoli. "Yes, with extra fortune cookies, please."

"You in, Leah?" Daddy asks once she hangs up. He shuffles one of the decks, his eyes still on the cards. Mama sighs again, but I know that sigh. She's going to say yes! I smile to myself.

"One round. Just one." She holds her finger up to make sure we all know what *one* means. But that finger doesn't hide the hint of a smile. It's not deep down from her toes, but it's enough. She sits, claiming her favorite, Scarlet. We play by the old rules, which means she'll go first.

In dreams and in life, nothing is impossible. Not even maybe, just maybe, getting my parents to change their minds before making a huge mistake.

CHAPTER 12

☆

Smooth as Butter

Serious trouble will bypass you.

It's seven a.m. Cardinals and mockingbirds whistle and shriek, but I don't hear a single wood thrush. The sun is already up, coloring the clouds with golden-red streaks. In the middle of the cottony puffs are rivers of blue. It is beautiful up there in the sky. It seems impossible for things to be so ugly right here, underneath.

Daddy's leaving.

Even though we had fun last night. Even though Mama joined in the game, they are still sticking to their plan. Time is up. Almost.

"It's a trial separation," Mama keeps saying. They

wanna try it out. They are putting the separation on trial, and at the end, they, the jury, will decide the verdict. I don't get a vote. Even though it's my life, too, I don't get to help decide.

At least that's what they think.

I have not given up yet, and I will at least make it hard for them to present their case. I am hiding Daddy's keys.

He pushes the button to unlock his white Jeep and leaves the keys dangling on the rack beside the garage door. Mama is in and out the room. The way she flits around, I can tell she doesn't wanna seem too helpful, like she's kicking Daddy out. But she also doesn't want it to look like she doesn't care at all. She keeps eyeing me, probably to see how I'm doing. Since I know she's looking for clues, I hide my real feelings.

I'm mad. I'm sad. But right now I'm mostly nervous that I'll get caught.

She leaves the room again, and as soon as Daddy puts his suitcase in the car, I snatch his keys and stash them in the refrigerator, in the butter compartment. It's a little shelf with a drawer—nothing really fits in there but butter. Butter, and now, Daddy's keys.

Just as I walk back toward the door, Mama returns to the kitchen. Daddy stands in the doorway, one foot in the house, one foot out. Mama inches closer. I'm not sure how we're supposed to say goodbye. This is why she wanted me at band camp, so I wouldn't be here for this moment.

I should be here, but this moment should not. According to my fortune, serious trouble should be bypassing me. My parents should be staying together and working things out, not "trying" separation. Daddy's brown eyes are full of sadness. Mama's are, too. And even though I'm trying to hide my feelings, I know theirs both mirror mine. If everyone is sad, isn't this a bad idea?

He reaches past me to grab his keys off the rack. They aren't there. He pats down his pockets.

"What's wrong?" asks Mama.

"My keys. They were right there."

"Did you put them in the car?"

"No, I don't think so." He goes to the driver's side to check. "Nope."

I stand still, not sure if I should pretend to look or not.

"Where was the last place you remember them?" Mama asks.

"The last place I remember them is . . . right here." He slows down, and I can hear the puzzle pieces slipping into place. My eyes follow his finger as he points to the key rack. "I stood here with the keys still on the rack and unlocked my car door. Just the way I always do."

He looks at me now. Mama does, too.

"Maya, did you take his keys?"

I didn't expect this direct question, and I'm not sure what to say. I don't say anything.

"Answer me. Where are your daddy's keys?"

"I don't have them," I say, which is literally true.

"Where did you put them?" She begins to open cabinets and drawers.

Watching her opening and closing things, looking for the keys, sets me on fire.

"You don't have to leave!" I shout.

"Maya." I hear Mama's warning tone.

"Nobody asked me!"

"I know this is hard, but please stop yelling," she says, voice sharpening.

"How come you guys aren't yelling? You're both quiet like it's a normal day. Like Daddy's going to the store or something, instead of starting a trial separation." I say *trial separation* with extra force, rolling my neck. I might get put on punishment, but I don't care.

We all stand there, near the open door, the warm June air circling around us. Even though it's still early, beads of sweat are forming on Daddy's bald head. Mama's arms are folded across her chest, the same way I fold mine when I'm trying to keep my feelings inside.

"Will you tell me where my keys are? Please?"

His tender tone melts my resolve. I sigh and point toward the fridge. He looks confused at first, then snickers and shakes his head. He flings open both doors and skims the insides. He sees them in the butter compartment, and his snicker turns into a laugh.

"I see. Stopping me *cold*, huh, MJ?"

The teeniest hint of a smile breaks free from my hot face. Mama groans. "Really, Mat?"

He takes a deep breath as I chew on my upper lip. *Stay, stay, stay,* I think loud enough for everyone to hear. But it doesn't work.

He steps toward me and I step back, crossing my arms. He gives me a look, pleading to make this easier. But I don't wanna make it easier. I want him to stay.

"What about your sourdough?"

He exhales. "I tossed it."

I gasp. He really is leaving.

"Don't go!" My voice cracks. "Mama!" I grab her hands, begging her to change her mind.

He pulls me to him then, wrapping me in a huge hug.

"You can't leave, Daddy!" I say through his shirt. "What if you decide you like it better without us? What if you don't come back?" I burst into tears then. Wailing.

He squeezes me tighter, and I smell the frankincense he wears every day. Mama rubs my back and sighs, but she doesn't say anything. She doesn't change her mind.

"MJ, I love you. There's no place I'd rather be than with my favorite girls," he says, holding me. "Remember, it's only eight weeks. And you'll see me. I'll take you to camp every other time. I'll be at your games, of course. Plus my new place isn't far. You can come anytime you want. And you still have your tablet—I'm just a video call away."

"I want you to stay."

He lifts my chin. His big brown eyes are pools of tears, but none of his tears escape and run down his face the way mine do. He hugs me once more. "You're always my MVP," he whispers in my ear.

"I love you, Leah," he says to Mama. "I hope the space . . . you know."

She nods and turns away from him. From us.

He rubs his nose against mine and gets into his car. He starts the engine, and the white Grand Cherokee roars to life. My stomach flutters in a wave of panic. As the big car drives away, I run after him, screaming, begging, "Please, Daddy, don't leave! Mama, make him stay! Don't let him leave."

She grabs me and pulls me back into the house. I want to snatch away from her so she can't touch me at all, but instead I cry into her. "Let him come back!" I sob, sob, sob.

"I'm sorry, Maya," she whispers as she squeezes me into her. "I really am. I just . . . We just need some time apart."

She sounds like she's sorry. She looks it, too. But deep down, I know she could stop this nightmare if she really, truly wanted to.

I drag myself to my room. I walk into the Cave, step into my sleeping bag, and hide away from everything.

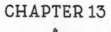

CHAPTER 13

Hot Now

**You find beauty in ordinary
things. Appreciate this gift.**

*D*ing *dong.*

The doorbell wakes me up. I scrub dried tears from my face, wondering who it might be. Daddy wouldn't ring the doorbell to his own house. That would be the worst. Maybe it's Ginger.

I step out of the closet and press my ear against my door. My heart stops when I hear Daddy's voice! I fling the door open, but as I keep listening, I realize it's not him after all. Mama is explaining that I am upset because "Mat's gone" and I took it "very hard." So it *was* Daddy's voice, only it was coming from Uncle Jimmy.

Maybe I am taking it "very hard," but watching your daddy leave should not be easy if you love him. If he loves you, too, and tells you every day with board games, cakes, and soccer. I spin the Wheel and stare at the fortune. *You find beauty in ordinary things. Appreciate this gift.* There's nothing beautiful or ordinary going on right now. It's just the opposite. The more I think about it, the sadder I feel. I am not sure what to do with all of these feelings, so for now I just feel them and try not to scream. I sneak to the top of the stairs.

"You need anything?" Uncle Jimmy asks Mama.

"Yeah, I need you to take these trophies."

"Which ones? Mat's?"

"Yeah. But I'm just kidding."

"Ha. I'm surprised he didn't take a couple."

"You and me both."

"If they bother you that much, I can take them."

"No. They can stay. They just . . . remind me of things I'd rather forget."

Not only is Daddy gone, she wants his trophies gone, too? What's the big deal? She doesn't like soccer, she doesn't like Daddy. Does she even like me? I rub my eyes as hard as I can, to stop new tears from falling.

"MJ!" Uncle Jimmy calls out from below.

I take my time walking downstairs, arms folded across my chest. I freeze when I see him. I know they are identical twins, but it's still a shock. Mama and Uncle Jimmy standing there looking a little too much like Mama with Daddy.

I look over at Mama and feel heat rising, overwhelming my sadness. I know in my bones this is all her fault. She doesn't want his trophies here. She didn't even want *me* here. She wanted me at camp.

"What are you up to, lil girl?" Uncle J asks.

I shake my head.

"Well, why don't you come and ride with me?"

I'm hot now.

Fiery mad, or maybe fiery sad, and it's June in Georgia, so I am sweating in Uncle Jimmy's car. He drives a Jeep, like Daddy does, only his is a bright yellow Wrangler instead of a white Grand Cherokee. Jazz pours from his speakers. I recognize the *Soul* soundtrack.

Today he has the top off, and the morning

sunshine warms my arms as the breeze whips around. The wind is nice, but I am still hot. I keep the heat all bottled up inside and stew silently in my seat, watching the houses and trees blur as we zoom by. Just as we leave the neighborhood, I spot Chaos. No teeth around his neck today. He's wearing bright blue swim trunks covered with pineapples and carrying a Popsicle-shaped raft. He must be going to the pool for opening day. I wanna go, but I don't feel like seeing anyone else today.

Uncle Jimmy turns the music down and finally speaks.

"I know you're upset, MJ."

It's not a question, so I don't give an answer. He waits before starting again.

"Wanna talk about it?"

"No."

He nods and turns the music back up, driving with one hand, looking cool and relaxed. Daddy's face bobbing along to the music. Daddy's voice asking me if I wanna talk about Daddy leaving.

I suck my teeth when I hear the piano jumping around. I love music, but I hate jazz solos. I never know who is about to do what and it's annoying. Why can't everyone stick to a melody? I want to know what's coming next. I am not in the mood for constant surprises. After a while my anger and annoyance and confusion all bubble up to the top.

"I hate them," I say into the wind and the music I can't stand. I can't tell whether or not he hears me because he doesn't flinch or stop or anything. He just drives, bobbing his head as if that were a part of the song he was expecting. But he's too mellow and I'm too upset, so I turn the music all the way off and demand, much louder now, "Did you hear me?"

"I did." He nods.

"I said I hate them." I snarl and ball my fists, trying to be dramatic like the parts in the music I don't like. "Why do they get to decide all this without me? What if I don't want anyone to divorce or separate or whatever they're doing? What if I want everything to stay the same?"

He breathes. Still listening to this part of the song. My solo. Waiting on his cue to join in. I slump low in my seat.

"Change is a part of life, MJ."

"Grown-ups always say that."

"It's always true."

"They're messing up everything. My summer. My life. Everything is all wrong now."

"It seems impossible," he says, "but you can still have a great summer. And a great life. I bet you've seen a fortune cookie like that." He clears his throat and pretends to recite a fortune. "Your summer outlook is wonderful. Better days are ahead."

I roll my eyes.

"I know it's hard, MJ. You're right to be upset about it. But he's still in town—he's just not in the same house. And there's always me. I do kind of look like him, don't you think? Except I'm better-looking, of course."

Any other day, I would've smiled at that.

"Is there something you want to say or ask? You know I'm up for it."

There's lots I wanna say or ask, but I don't wanna hear "You're too young to understand" or anything like that. To be on the safe side, I just say no. He nods and turns the music back on. A new song is playing. I stare out the window, getting lost in my feelings, ignoring the music before it dances on my nerves.

I pay attention when I feel the car slowing, turning into a shopping plaza. We are pulling up to a Krispy Kreme. The HOT NOW sign is lit up, and a line of cars is forming in the drive-through. My eyes grow round with shock. When it's our turn to order, Uncle

Jimmy says in that deep, honey-coated voice he and Daddy share, "Half a dozen glazed." Except Daddy would *never* say that.

My mouth hangs open.

"What?" he says.

"You're getting doughnuts," I whisper in shock.

"What else do people get at Krispy Kreme?"

"But . . . Daddy."

"What about him?"

I feel a giggle coming up, but I'm not ready to let one out. "He always says don't buy it if you can bake it."

"Hold this."

He hands me the warm box while he asks for extra napkins. I stare at it, knowing the deliciousness inside. The smell of the glazed sugar makes my mouth water. It's been forever since I've had one, but you never forget.

"Listen. My brother is decent—decent at barbecue. And he's really masterful at baking. But no one is beating Krispy Kreme glazed. HOT NOW? Stop playing."

I laugh and put a warm, soft ring into a napkin, into his hand, and take one for myself.

We click the doughnuts together in a toast, although there's nothing at all to celebrate. He seems to know what I'm thinking when he says, "MJ, even in the middle of pain, there's always sweetness if you know where to look."

CHAPTER 14

⭐

Marco?

You will do well to expand
your horizons.

Uncle J drops me off, and I enter a quiet house. No
fun music blasting and no funny Daddy joking.
Just Mama in her room with her door closed and now
me in mine.

To break the silence, I look up Nestor Torres, a
jazz flautist that Uncle J promised I'd like. He wanted
me to hear "Let There Be Light." I find it in no time
and press play. It starts off sort of like a march, but
then it immediately smooths when a Spanish guitar
joins in. Can a song be upbeat and mellow at the same
time? After a while I feel myself being swept away in

the music, fingering an air flute. By the end, everything slows down, like sunset. In the silence, I float
back down, remembering I am still sad.

"Now what?" I ask my Wheel. I spin and spin and
spin it around. Every time it slows to stop, I spin it
again. Where's my fortune saying Daddy will be back
soon?

I spin, wishing for good news, a glimmer of hope,
something. Around and around, the fortunes and the
blue paint become a blurry mess just like I feel.

"Hey!"

I jump, startled to hear Ginger.

"You missed my messages?"

I look around and spot my tablet on the floor,
using the time to "fix my face" as Mama would say.
I'm not ready to let anyone know something's wrong.
Not even Ginger.

I turn to explain I've been out with Uncle Jimmy,
but stop when I see Angelica. *Why did she have to
come, too?*

"We're going to the pool! It's open!"

I remember Chaos this morning, sporting his pine-
apple shorts. So much has happened already today.

I'm not in the mood to go with them, but I don't
want to stay in the quiet house, either. I change into

a suit and sneak a look at the Wheel since I never saw where it landed. *You will do well to expand your horizons.* I shrug and then tell Mama where we're headed. We set off, loaded down with sunscreen and towels and snacks.

When we arrive, the three of us stop and stare. It's not just a new pool, it's a whole new complex. There's a concession-style window where you check in. There's tables and benches in a covered area—a cabana. The pool looks enormous through the new iron fence.

Ms. Shae, a plump-cheeked woman with glittery blue stiletto nails, greets us.

"Hi, girls! Do you know the new rules?" she asks.

"No, ma'am." We shake our heads.

She points to the rules posted beside her window and explains that kids under thirteen must wear a bracelet at all times. To get a green bracelet, you must pass the deep water test. Kids who haven't passed wear a yellow bracelet and stay away from the deep end. Little kids have to wear red ones and stay with their parents. We nod as she fastens yellow bracelets on our wrists, scans them, and types our names into her tablet.

Once we're past the gate, we plop down our stuff and ease our way into the middle of the pool. Not too close to the shallow end to look like babies, but not near the deep, so we don't get in trouble. Ginger and Angelica talk about "getting their greens."

A boy I don't recognize yells "Marco!" and leaps smack-dab into the deep. Before he disappears underwater, I spot his green bracelet. There are only a couple of other greens so far. A few kids yell "Polo!" back and they start playing.

I stare. The deep end is *really* deep. Eight feet? That's almost two of me! Is this what expanding my horizons means? A pang of terror blooms in my chest. This is nothing like the other pool.

I look around, but no one else seems concerned about "getting their green." It's hard to picture treading in that deep water or doing whatever else I have to do to get a green. My stomach sinks. I love to master things, but who knows when I'll master this? I might be stuck at yellow for a while. One more thing to worry about this summer.

"Soccer camp starts Monday!" sings Ginger. "I wonder who else is going?"

"I don't know, but my cousin says soccer camps like the one we're doing are the *only* way to get off the rec teams like the Astros and play for real," says Angelica.

"I still don't get how it really helps," Ginger says.

"Soccer ID camps are just for scouting. Most of the time we have regular practices and scrimmages. But . . ." Angelica leans in and lowers her voice. We lean in, too. "The club coaches come and watch us. *Especially* the exhibition games. That's when the clubs decide who they're gonna invite to try out. Well, everybody except Ginger. Miss MVP won't have to worry about her invite." She wiggles her fingers at Ginger, who blushes in protest.

"Stop! We all have to play our best. And anyway, trying out doesn't mean you make the team. It just means you have a chance."

"That's true." Angelica nods. "*All* the good teams will be there."

I imagine the closing exhibition. Daddy on the sidelines, cheering with all his might. If the Chargers invite me to try out, he will be so happy. A wave of sadness rushes over me. *Why did he have to leave? Why are they trying separation?*

Ginger thumps my ribs underwater. When I look up, she mouths, "What's wrong?" I smooth away my frown and shake my head. I can't talk about it in front of Angelica. But that reminds me—Ginger still has something to tell me, too.

Someone yells "Volleyball!" and a floatable net makes its way to the middle of the pool.

"Now we're talking! Let's go kick some butt!" yells Angelica as she swims over to the net. Ginger and I follow, and the other kids pick sides. I'm glad we're on the shallow end.

I don't know how or when I'll "get my green." But I do know I'll be the best player at soccer camp. That's the least I can do for Daddy while we're separated. Be the best baller I can be and earn myself a spot as a Charger.

CHAPTER 15

☆

No Questions

Your luck will surface in
unexpected ways.

"What's that?" Mama asks when I get back home
from the pool. She pulls my wrist to inspect
the bright yellow bracelet.

"We have to wear this until we pass a deep water
test, and then we get a green one."

"Oh. I did see a notice about that. Well, when do
you want to take the test?"

I shrug, annoyed. I reach for my stuff, ready to go
change clothes. But she tries again.

"Well, pick a date. You have the basics down. You

just need a week to practice. A couple at most. I can teach you in no time."

"You?" I blurt out.

"Yes, Maya. Me." Her cool tone chills the air. *She's* annoyed now. But I'm shocked by this whole conversation. She sounds so casual, like our lives didn't just get turned upside down! And does she even really swim? She used to come with Ginger and me to the pool sometimes, but I can't remember her in the water. She was always sunbathing with a book.

"I've never seen you swim."

"You've never seen me do a lot of things." She purses her lips and turns to her book, but I can see her eyes aren't really moving. After a while she stops "reading" and looks over at me.

"I can swim," she says, calmer now. Quiet, almost as if she doesn't want anyone else to hear. "I just . . . haven't in a long time. I can teach you." She shifts in her seat and takes a deep breath. I wait for whatever she's planning to say next.

"Maya, I know everything happened really fast last night. This morning. Are you ready to talk about it? Do you have any questions yet?"

Everyone keeps asking me if I have questions. Yes,

I have questions. What are the "lot of things" I've never seen her do? What does she have against soccer? The more serious I get about it, the less she likes it. Why is that? And why did her light dim this year? Was it her darkness that made Daddy leave? Will he really be back at the end of summer? Does she think teaching me how to swim will make me forget he's gone?

The longer I stand here, the longer my list grows, and the angrier I feel. I don't know why she smiles less, but I do know that Daddy is gone because she wanted him gone. It was her idea. I heard her with my own ears that night. *Maybe it's best if you leave,* she'd said.

I don't really want to know about all the things she can do. I don't want her to teach me how to swim. It doesn't matter that she doesn't like soccer. Daddy loves it and so do I. The only thing that matters is that they promised he'd be back in eight weeks, and I'm already counting down. When he comes back, I'll be a brand-new Charger. I'll have a new royal blue jersey with *MJ* on the back.

She watches as I grab my things to head up to my room.

"No, I don't have any questions."

CHAPTER 16

Something to Prove

Nothing can keep you from
reaching your goals. Do it!

Mama and Daddy will alternate taking me to camp. It's Mama's turn first. We check in early enough for me to do my 500 touches before things kick off. I want to do whatever it takes the next few weeks to make sure I get a serious look from the Chargers. There's nothing I can do about that MVP trophy, but as Daddy would say, *A setback is just a setup for a comeback.*

It feels good to be out here on the fields. I love the warm sunshine on my shoulders. Band camp might've been a lot of fun, I admit to myself, but soccer is more important right now. I inhale the scent of onions from the just-cut grass, tune in to the birds singing in the nearby trees, and begin counting off my touches.

By the time the other campers assemble on the sidelines, my touches are done and I'm jumping up and down, a ball of energy ready to break free. Deep down, I'm nervous. I'm never nervous about soccer, but I really don't want anything else to go wrong. I smile and wave at the other girls. Many of them were Astros, including Ginger and Angelica, but there are new faces, too. I look around before we get started, half hoping Daddy will yell out, "Let's go play some footballlllll!" But of course he's not here.

Instead, Coach Jayme blows her whistle. She's tall and sturdy. She reminds me more of a professional basketball player than a soccer coach. I can tell by the way she holds her whistle just near her mouth, eyeing us one by one from underneath her white visor, that she will not spend the next three weeks smiling and cracking jokes with us. We're about to work.

After introductions, we start drills and conditioning. We're a little rusty even though we've only had a few days off. Lots of bad technique and running after loose balls at first. Lots of whistle-blowing to hurry us back into formation. When it seems we finally remember the basics, she lines us up to scrimmage so she can get an idea of how we all play. Soon enough, I'm tuned in. I already know how my old teammates flow, and the new ones aren't hard to figure out. My team draws first blood. Then a few minutes later we score again.

After a while, I can't help but notice a few dark looks and huffs in my direction. Even Ginger scrunches her nose. We're scoring and I'm handling the ball well, so I don't know why they're acting funny. Suddenly Angelica blocks me from the ball and kicks it over to Ashley, which is exactly what I was about to do. "MJ, you're not the only one here!" she hisses as she jogs past me. *What is that supposed to mean?* I scowl as a flame ignites in my chest. I jump in place to calm down.

During the water break, Angelica towers over me and says, loud enough for everyone to hear, "It's the first day—you don't have to be so extra." I grip the bleachers so I don't stand up and cause an even bigger scene, but I really want to shout her down.

I spot other eyes looking at the ground or staring hard at their cups. The same way Mama did when she didn't want to meet my eyes to confirm the bad news. *What gives? I'm just trying to do my best. Aren't we all?*

As everyone heads back to the field, Ginger whispers to me, "We're supposed to be a team. It's not all about you, MJ."

I frown at her, but I keep quiet. Some things *are* all about me. I'm the one who lost the Golden Astro to her best friend. I'm the one whose daddy just moved out. I'm the one who has to do *something* to make everything right again.

Losing MVP wasn't up to me. Watching Daddy drive away wasn't up to me. But doing my best for the next four weeks? That part is up to me. Even my fortune this morning said: *Nothing can keep you from reaching your goals. Do it!* If the Charger scouts don't notice me, it won't be because I didn't give my all.

Coach blows a warning whistle. Time is just about up. I sigh. What if Daddy doesn't come back at the end of the summer? If I make the team, at least he and I will still have soccer.

I want to grab Ginger's hand. To pull her back and explain. Instead, I watch her dash back to the field. Without me.

CHAPTER 17

☆

Music Lesson

Better to ask twice than lose
yourself once.

Uncle J pulls up just as camp is finishing. "Blinding Lights" by The Weeknd seeps out the windows and surrounds his Jeep. Ginger and I both hop into the back. He turns down the music and asks us about the first day. This part is supposed to be easy. Stories about the coach, the old heads, the new girls. The first-day mistakes. But neither of us has much to say.

Well, I do. I want to tell her about Daddy and explain why I was trying so hard today. I want to ask her what was wrong the other day, if everything is okay now. I want to know if she's upset with me for wishing I had won the Golden Astro.

But I can't say all that in front of Uncle Jimmy.

"Y'all must be tired."

"Coach is cool," I finally say.

"Yeah, she's all right," Ginger says, turning to me. "She's strict, but I think camp will be fun." She doesn't look upset, but her eyes are faraway, like maybe she's thinking about something else.

"Whatcha doing the rest of the day?" I ask as we pull up to her house.

"Pa Pa is coming over again. We're supposed to go out to dinner." She opens her mouth to say something else, but when she sees Uncle J watching in the rearview mirror, she changes her mind. "I'll tell you later," she says quietly.

"Don't forget."

"I won't. Thanks for the ride, Uncle Jimmy," she says, waving goodbye.

I get up front for the short ride down to my house. When he parks, I sit there, not reaching for the door. I don't want to get out yet. Mama is at work for a little while longer, and Daddy is . . . gone.

"You need anything?"

"No."

"So . . . what's up? How was the first day? Really?"

"It was okay. Some of the girls think I was doing too much, like trying too hard."

"Were you?" His eyebrows rise with the question.

"I was trying to do a good job, yeah. But I don't think it was too much. I just need to . . . stand out this summer."

He rubs his goatee for a while, nodding his head although he isn't answering a question or listening to any music.

"Is it time for a break?"

"From what?"

"I know you wanted that trophy, and now my brother's moved out for a few weeks. It's a lot for a kid. It's okay if you just want to have fun and do something besides soccer this summer."

"Soccer *is* fun."

"Is it?"

I never get mad at Uncle Jimmy, but I guess there's a first time for everything. I pretend to scratch something off my palm so I can ignore the prickle of heat.

"MJ, are you a good listener?"

"Yes."

"Alright. Listen to this."

"Is it jazz?" I'm definitely not in the mood for one

of those songs where people do things I'm not expecting. He stares at me like my nose is on backward.

"Excuse me?"

"I don't . . . really love jazz."

"Stop it."

"I mean, some songs are cool. I liked Nestor Torres, but his style is different. Some jazz is, I don't know, confusing."

"MJ!"

"Uncle J!"

"Why are you doing this to me?"

"Doing what?"

"Breaking my heart!" he shouts dramatically, clutching his chest and throwing his head back on his car seat.

"I'm not!"

"You are! What's your name?"

"Maya."

"Um. Your whole name?"

"Maya Jenkins. *MJ* for short."

"All of it."

"Maya Jazzmine Jenkins," I say slowly.

"Maya Jazzmine. Two *z*'s." He flashes the deuce sign. "Dos."

"I always wondered about that."

"Wonder no more. I gave you that name."

"Really?"

"Yes! You're my niece and goddaughter, and I love music and I love you. So I brought everything together in beautiful harmony. Jazzmine," he says with extra mustard on the *z*'s.

"Oh," I giggle.

He presses play. The song is one I've never heard before. It starts quietly at first with what sounds like brushes on a drum, and then suddenly it fills up the whole car with a funky African music sound. After a minute or so, he turns it down again. I nod, really impressed.

"Now." He locks eyes with me. "What's the fourth instrument you hear?"

I frown and make a *Really?* face at him.

"It's not a memory test. I'm playing it again. Fourth instrument. Listen."

He restarts it.

"Oh, it's a flute."

"Sure?" He chuckles and plays it again.

"Oh. Well, now I think it's a triangle. There's a lot happening in that song."

He points at me like I said something important and nods.

"One more time. Fourth instrument."

He turns it up and I lean toward the speakers, eyes closed, concentrating. "Oh!" I point as soon as it comes in. "It's definitely the triangle. Right?"

"You got it!" We high-five. I didn't even hear the triangle at all the first two times. But it's definitely there.

"How did you finally hear that triangle?"

"I listened." I shrug, not sure what he's getting at.

"Yes. You knew there was something else to hear, so you tried harder. Look! I even took a picture of you."

He turns his phone to me and I see me there. Random strands from my cornrows frizzy and flying, eyes closed, nose practically smelling the speaker. I'm frowning, but not sad or mad, just concentrating.

"Oh," I say, studying the photo. "Is this about soccer?"

"It's about everything. You have your own thoughts and feelings about things. I just want you to listen to them. Listen to your own songs. Sometimes it means tuning everything and everyone out, so you can really tune in to *you*." He points to his head and his chest.

"Can you hear other people's songs?"

"Mm-hmm. We can tune in to each other. Sometimes, well *usually*, you have to try more than once, but we can hear them."

"Do Mama and Daddy hear each other's songs?"

"I don't know, MJ. That, I don't know."

CHAPTER 18

☆

Too Much to Tackle

The near future holds a gift of contentment.

It's still dark when I wake up, but I'm too excited to go back to sleep. It's been four whole days since I've seen Daddy, and it's his turn to take me to soccer! I tiptoe over to the Cave and pull out Flicker. When I'm ready, I play my current favorite, *The Barber of Seville*. I'm still not that great at it yet, but even slow and on Quiet Mode, it makes me laugh. My fingers get a little faster as I repeat the fun phrases over and over again. At first I think we should do a soccer highlight reel with this in the background. But the more I try to picture it, the more I realize it sounds like a bunch of running around and missing the goal. *Maybe not a great idea*, I chuckle to myself.

After a while, I put my flute away and get ready for camp. I peer out the window. Despite the cheerful music and my good mood, it's the dreariest morning ever—hazy and gray outside. It's definitely gonna storm later. I close my eyes, concentrate on a great day of soccer, and spin the wheel. It lands on: *The near future holds a gift of contentment.* I give it two thumbs-up. *Contentment* means happiness, and Daddy is on his way.

When he pulls up, Daddy is a ray of sunshine. I leap into the back seat, but stretch up front to cover his smooth face with noisy kisses. He has finally cut off his beard. "There's my babygirl!" he shouts, laughing between smooches. I smile, inhaling his frankincense as he drives three doors down.

Ginger jumps in, chatting about the weather, wondering if we'll still get to play today's scrimmage against another camp. I hope so. I don't know if the club coaches come to the scrimmages, but if they do, I'll be ready.

Daddy asks Ginger how she's been, if anything is new with her. Something is, although I still don't know what. I stick my arm out the window, letting my hand ride the roller coaster of air. The whooshing almost feels good enough to drown out the tightness building in my chest. Something's new with me, too. Ginger still has no idea Daddy moved out for the summer. It's only been a few days, and it just hasn't been the right time to tell her. And right now is definitely the wrong time.

Deep down, I feel as though telling her will make it true, and I'm still not ready to believe it. I feel guilty for keeping it secret, but I laugh and chat with them to play it off.

It's all over too fast. When Daddy parks, Ginger hops out and waves goodbye. To her, it's just another ride in a thousand rides, but to me it's a stolen moment. I kiss him goodbye and stand there, squeezing the truth as far from the light of day as I can, down, down, down into the pit of my stomach. But the seed of sadness is already blooming.

He merges in behind the other parents and follows the long driveway out of the park. I stare as his car gets smaller and smaller. Maybe Mama was right that I should've gone to band camp. Right about now I would probably be practicing a brand-new song. *Maybe even jazz.* I almost smile at that. I wave away

the raindrops just beginning to land on my face and
jog to the field to catch up with everyone else.

During the game, the rain is a steady drum and I am
distracted, wondering if Daddy will really move back
home seven weeks from now. I miss an easy pass from
Angelica. Then I miss another one. "MJ!" she yells.

Shut! Up! In my mind I yell at the top of my lungs,
loud enough to drown out the rain and the soccer
game and everything else a mile away. I imagine I
shout it so loud that I am hoarse for days after, but
everyone knows to leave me alone. I hate, hate, hate
to be yelled at! Especially today, when my heart is
already aching. I ball my fists so tight, my nails dig
into my palms.

Sadness and heat churn to lava inside me, threat-
ening to erupt. I want to sit down. To cool off. To
quiet the voices in my head. To erase the surprised
looks from my team. Instead I shake my arms and
bounce around, trying to look ready for action.

Ginger catches my eye. She throws her hands out
to ask what's going on. I look up and let the rain fall
on my face. It's getting heavier, but it's not enough to

stop the game. We have a few minutes left, so I still have time to redeem myself.

Finally, I win the ball. I even see a clear line to the goal. "Man on!" someone yells. I run, slipping, and just when I am about to pass, *whoosh*, an opponent slides for a tackle. Down I go with her. She barely touches me, but that light scrape is the final trigger. I flop around grabbing my leg, screaming out in pain that it hurts. But really, it's my heart that hurts. I know the clock is running, but I can't stop rocking back and forth, rolling myself into a ball. The only thing making me feel better is knowing the club coaches didn't come today. There's no one in royal blue and gold watching this disaster.

I open my eyes when a chorus of voices approaches. Are they annoyed? Angry? Professional soccer players are known to flop around, trying to get penalties called on the opposing team. Coach wouldn't be happy if she thought I was faking it. She leans over me to investigate. I'm not. I am crying—real, fat tears, bigger than the raindrops still falling. I feel better crying. Freer at least.

Curiosity on her face dissolves into concern. "Where does it hurt?" asks one of the trainers. She means my leg or foot or wherever the pain is. But it hurts everywhere and nowhere anyone can see.

They help me up, and I limp over muddy puddles to the bench. People are clapping, glad I'm okay enough to walk on my own power. Coach subs Ginger out, too, and she plops down beside me. I think of the pictures in the closing banquet video. The ones where we are side by side, our arms thrown around each other.

I miss her. I miss talking to her without Angelica around. I miss being a good friend. Even though she does not ask what's wrong, I'll bet she knows it's not about soccer. She scoots closer to me, so her arm touches mine. I finally look at her, study her freckly cheeks, wet from the rain. I see something familiar but out of place on her face. She seems sad, too. She still hasn't told me her secret.

"What happened?" a trainer asks, trying to figure out if I need ice or a bandage or what. *My daddy moved out.*

"I think we just slid wrong. The mud." Everyone understands sliding and legs going the wrong way and pain like that.

Mama comes to pick me up early. The rain has stopped, but everything is still gray. Coach, in her no-nonsense way, tells her about the play. That I cried at first but shook it off, and that was that. I can tell from the way Mama looks at me, relieved, that she thinks the storm—my storm—has passed. That whatever happened was only about soccer, and everything is fine now.

At home, she calls Daddy to let him know about camp. That she had to pick me up. "Coach said she was distracted and playing poorly. And then this tackle sent her over the edge. But after that . . ."

I shake my head and ignore the rest of what she says. She doesn't get it. I'm not over the edge. I am just brokenhearted.

CHAPTER 19

☆

Daddy's Daisies

Don't give up. The beginning is
always hardest.

The doorbell rings and soon I hear Daddy's voice.
My heart races, but I tell myself not to get
excited. It could be Uncle Jimmy again. I crack my
door open and hear him saying something about me
being chatty when he dropped me off this morning.
It's definitely Daddy.

I run downstairs two at a time. It feels like it has
been forever since I've seen him, not just a few hours.
He gives me one of his big bear hugs. I relax into him
and inhale.

"I hear you were out for the count!" he booms, smiling down at me.

I nod, feeling my cheeks warm in embarrassment.

"Had everyone out there worried. Even me, and I wasn't there to see it!" He chuckles and I hide my face in his shirt.

"You feeling better now?" he asks, pulling away to inspect me. "You got down those steps pretty fast, so I'm guessing you do!" He winks, coaxing a smile from my lips.

"I brought you something." He points to a small, clear cake box gift-wrapped with a royal blue bow. Inside I spy a thick slice of white cake with white icing. It's sitting in the middle of the kitchen table along with a mason jar of my favorite flowers, gerbera daisies. It all makes the once empty table seem much more cheerful now.

"You don't have to eat those *store-bought* doughnuts your uncle likes." He laughs at his own joke. "Don't buy it if—what?" He points at me.

"You can bake it," I finish, laughing. "Thank you!" I kiss him on the cheek, and he grabs my hand, striding toward the door. "You're already leaving?"

"I just came to say hello. Sounds like you were having a hard time."

I nod as the sadness creeps back in.

"I love you," he says. "Don't forget."

I nod again.

"And watch out for those tackles! You have an exhibition match coming up. Need a cheerleader?"

"Definitely!"

"You got it! Thanks for keeping me in the loop, Leah." He lowers his voice and asks, "Need anything?"

Mama looks back at him like she's not sure how to answer, but finally she says, "No, I'm fine, Mat. Thank you."

"Got it." Daddy nods. We nose kiss, and away he goes, much too soon. I run to the door and wave until it's impossible for him to see me anymore.

Just like that, the sadness fills all the way to the top again, and I stand there, not knowing what to do with it all. It's too much for one person, and I feel full to bursting when I close the door.

"Why can't he stay?"

Mama sighs and pulls me to her. I want to jerk away and run, to scream and cry. But I stand there anyway. She smooths my hair back and kisses my forehead, something she hasn't done in forever. I want her to stop because it makes me feel better, and I don't wanna feel better. I wanna be mad at her until he comes back. After all, it's her fault he's gone.

"I know you miss him. I know this is hard. It's just a few more weeks."

"Then he'll be back?"

"Then we'll see. Until then, you can talk to him whenever you want. You can even see him whenever you want."

"It's not the same."

"Maya."

It's the way she says it, with sharp edges even though my name is soft. I know she's going to say something I don't like. My anger boils back up, overtaking the sadness.

"Today was a bit of a scare, but he's not coming after every cut and scrape. If you want to see him, you can ask like—"

"Normal? It's not normal, Mama!" I shout, pulling away from her. "It's normal for Daddy to be here! Why do you want me to act like nothing is different? Everything is different! Everything!"

She sighs. I whirl around and run to my room as fast as my legs can go. I head straight to my Wheel and stare at it for what feels like hours. Today was supposed to be about happiness. Contentment in the near future. Maybe "near" is further away than I thought. After a while, I'm ready to try again. I take a deep breath and concentrate on Daddy and the near, far future. I spin, spin, spin the Wheel.

Don't give up. The beginning is always hardest.

I blink back tears, wishing I had thought to bring Daddy's daisies upstairs with me. I pull out my tablet and visit the Flute Girl Rocks channel. I play along to "Let It Go" into the night, until I fall asleep.

CHAPTER 20

⭐

I Like NY

You will soon gain something
you've always wanted.

"**N**ice shirt!" Uncle J nods and smiles at a skater rocking a white T-shirt with *I only like NY as a friend* across the front. The first week of soccer camp is over, and the two of us have finally made it to the park. It's Saturday morning, and we're among the few early birds here already. The man gives a two-finger salute and rolls on by.

"What's so great about his shirt?"

"Back in the day, the slogan was 'I love New York' with a big red heart you could see from a mile away. It's just funny. It's cool—he's doing his own thing."

Uncle J unzips his duffel bag and lays out a blanket. So far it's just us—his students haven't arrived yet. He fishes out his instruments. He's brought a few in case he wants to jump in and play: a clarinet, a cornet, and a cowbell.

"Those are all . . . totally different," I laugh.

"Exactly! I can play whatever I'm in the mood for or whatever the music needs right then."

"You never know when a song needs a cowbell?"

"Exactly. Or a triangle. Or a flute!" he says, giving me a look.

My face burns and I avoid his eyes. "I only like the flute as a friend," I lie.

"Ouch! You're breaking my heart."

I want to tell Uncle J about Flicker, but I don't know if he would keep my secret. He and Mama both would see it as ammunition to give up soccer, at least for now. And if Daddy found out, wouldn't he be disappointed I'm not giving soccer my all? It's better to keep it to myself.

"Sorry." I shrug.

"So what's new?"

"The pool is officially open! It's fancy."

"Tell me more!"

"It's big and now they have all these rules. Someone

has to check you in. You gotta take a deep water test and wear a green bracelet to show you passed. Ginger's getting hers right now."

"And you're here with your favorite uncle? Why didn't you tell me you wanted to do the swim test today? We can come to the park all summer long."

I look at him. He looks back at me, and his eyes grow round.

"Wait. You can swim, right?"

"I can do the basics, but . . . the water wasn't very deep at the old pool."

"Wow. I'm surprised Leah let you get away with that."

I look away at the mention of Mama's name.

"What's with that face?"

I suck my teeth. "I don't know."

"Come on, tell Uncle J."

"She just doesn't get me. She doesn't really like soccer. She even wanted me to go to . . . some other camp," I complain, leaving out the band part. "And it's all her fault that Daddy moved out for the summer," I say to the ground.

"What do you mean it's her fault? You don't know the whole story. No one does, except them. I'm sure she'd tell you more if you'd give her a chance."

It's her fault because it was her idea, I think as the heat rises in my chest. *I heard her tell him to leave.* I look away, plucking blades of grass instead of replying. Why is Uncle J taking her side anyway? Who is taking Daddy's side? Or mine?

A small group of teens arrive. They set up under the pink crape myrtles across from us. They must be his students because they wave in our direction when they spot Uncle J. He waves back.

"Talk to her. She probably gets you better than you think. And she will help you pass the swim test in no time."

"I've never seen Mama swim. Have you?"

He throws his head back at this one, like he really can't believe what he's hearing.

"What's so funny?" I say, watching him take forever to catch his breath.

"I was that age once," he says finally, pointing to the kids tuning their instruments. "Crisp haircut with fancy lines. All that. Can you picture it?"

"Sort of."

"So was your mom."

"I know . . ."

"Back then, your mother *lived* in the water. She's part mermaid! I can't believe you don't know this.

Ask her to show you the album."

"What album?"

"The green photo album. She'll know *exactly* what you mean."

I shake my head, but remain silent.

"Trust me, MJ, this is your mission. Find the green photo album and then pass that test."

"I don't really care about the test."

"Oh no?"

I shake my head once more, staring at his students. "Whether I pass or not, I can still go to the pool and hang out with my friends. Same as always."

"MJ, we talked about this. You're supposed to be listening to yourself." He tugs on his earlobe. "Really ask yourself what's true and *listen*."

I huff and return to picking blades of grass. I already know what's true—I *do* want to get a green bracelet. But not bad enough to let Mama help me.

My fortune says, *You will soon gain something you've always wanted*. More than anything else this summer, I want Daddy back home and to win a spot with the Chargers. Swimming is way back in third place.

CHAPTER 21

✩

Mission Impossible

All the efforts you are making will
ultimately pay off.

"**M**aya, is that you?" Mama calls out from the kitchen.

"Yes, ma'am."

"Had fun with Jimmy this morning?"

"Yeah."

"Good, good."

I stand in the foyer, still as a statue, hoping she won't ask more questions. I want to find the photo album since Uncle J insisted it was my "mission" at least two more times before we left the park. When she doesn't say anything else, I peek around the corner and see her head buried in a book.

If you can't find it when you get home, ask your mama where it is, he'd said. I'll look for it, but I haven't changed my mind about *asking* her for it. Uncle J guessed the album was in a storage bin or something. The only ones I know of are in Daddy's closet. I give her one last look and spin around as quietly as I can, then tiptoe my way up the stairs and down the hallway.

She keeps the bedroom door closed now, even when no one is in it. I pause to listen. The house is just so quiet lately. We always streamed music when Daddy was here—usually salsa or R&B. But nothing now. I turn the knob super slowly and give it a push. OMG! I freeze at the loud squeak. I listen to see if she's moving, but the sound of my heartbeat drowns out everything else.

Finally, I creep inside. It's strange—everything looks the same, but it seems empty without Daddy here. Quiet. Dark. I rush to the closet. If she walks in here now, I will have to explain what I'm doing.

The bin closest to me is full of sweaters and purses. The second one is packed with clothes I've outgrown, books I used to read, art supplies. I open the next one expecting more of the same. But when I lift up the top,

I nearly faint. It's filled with Daddy's shirts and sneakers. I yank out a black T-shirt and hold it up to me. It has a Darth Vader quote across the middle: *I AM YOUR FATHER.* It's too big, but I slip it on anyway. I pull out a brown one next. It says *MELANIN* and the formula for it in gold foil. I inhale the shirt, hoping to smell frankincense, any hint of Daddy at all. It's silly—these shirts were probably washed since he last wore them. But I inhale again anyway, as deep as I can.

"Maya?"

I jump. She sounds so close. And tense, the way parents sound when you don't answer the first time. I toss the *MELANIN* shirt back into the bin, shove everything like it was, and rush out into the hallway.

"Maya?"

"Yes, ma'am?" I know I sound breathless and guilty.

"What are you doing? Didn't you hear me calling you? I was asking if you're hungry."

She arrives at the top of the stairs with her detective eyes on. She takes one look at me and one look at her room. I've left the door wide open.

"What were you doing in my room?"

"It's not just *your* room!" The sudden flames leap out of my mouth, scorching the space between us.

"Excuse me?" she says, her own steam rising. "Watch your tone."

"It's Daddy's room, too," I say to the floor.

"Listen Maya, I miss him, too. But he —"

"No you don't!"

"I don't what?"

"You don't miss him," I insist, meeting her eyes now.

"You don't understand."

"Grown-ups always say that! But *you* did it! You made Daddy leave!" There. I finally said what I've been thinking all this time.

"Why would you say something like that?"

Her mouth falls open. She looks genuinely shocked, but I know it's all an act. I know the truth.

"I heard you that day." I point at her with laser-beam fingers. "I heard you with my own ears. You told him, 'Maybe it's best if you just leave.' It was YOUR idea." I squeeze my eyes and fists tight, tight, tight as she storms closer to me. I try to fight the tears, but I'm already losing.

She stands there forever in silence. Finally, she exhales. "You didn't hear everything. Let me explain."

She sounds flat and far away. I open my eyes and

she's looking toward the bedroom door, almost as if she's staring into another time and place.

"I heard that part," I choke out as my tears fall freely now. "The part where YOU told Daddy to leave! And now he's gone!"

I run past her, to where I should've been, my room.

"Maya," she says like she's pleading with me to talk to her.

"It's MJ!" I shout back. "Why can't you call me that like everyone else?"

As I close the door, I realize I still have on Daddy's T-shirt. I go straight for the Cave, to my sleeping bag, and snuggle deep inside. She knocks on my door and calls my name, *MJ* this time. But I don't answer and she doesn't come in. Eventually, she leaves me alone.

I cry hot, fat, I-hate-you tears until I am wrung all the way dry.

CHAPTER 22

The Sunshines

**You will have good luck in your
personal affairs.**

Imust've cried myself to sleep, because a couple of
hours later Ginger shakes me awake.

"Hey! What are you doing in here?" she asks,
leaning over me, peering around in the Cave. *Wishing
for good luck in my personal affairs,* I think to myself,
remembering the latest spin on my Wheel of Fortunes.

"I don't know. I fell asleep," I mumble. I stretch
my toes to feel for my flute case. It's still there, and
out of sight.

"Your face is all puffy."

I rub sleep from my eyes, but I don't explain,

hoping she will just breeze on like always. She doesn't let me down.

"Well, wake up! It's three o'clock! Wanna go to the pool with me and Angelica?"

Angelica? Again? I close my eyes so she won't see me rolling them. I'm annoyed, but even hanging with Angelica is better than being cooped up in my closet. I nod and push myself up.

"We got our greens this morning!" She wiggles her wrist at me. *We.*

"Was it hard?"

"The test? Nope! It took like five minutes. Plus if you go early, no one is really there yet. No audience. Ohh, pictures!" She spots the stack in the corner. "Are these the same ones I saw last time, or different ones?"

"Different ones."

She flips through them while I pull on my swim-suit and some shorts.

"Ohh, can I have these?" She waves two pictures of herself. They're both from a couple of years ago. She's playing soccer in one, and the other is a school picture. Her hair was all brushed down instead of parted down the middle and braided like it usually is.

"Yeah. Why?"

"I'm—it's for a project. I'm making something. I'll tell you about it. Later." Her cheeks flush red, but she doesn't say anything else. It's the third time she's promised "later." But I guess we're still even until I spill my own news.

We run into Chaos on our way to the pool. He's wearing swim trunks with palm trees and rubber ducks instead of pineapples this time, and he's walking down the street. The *middle* of the street. He's putting one foot in front of the other on the painted white line. He even has his arms out in a T, like he's balancing on a beam.

"What are you doing?" I call out to him from the sidewalk.

He looks around as if I could be talking to someone else. *Me?* he asks with his thumb and eyebrows.

"Yes," Ginger chimes in, smiling big.

"The same thing you're doing."

Now it's my turn to look around.

"Um, no, not really," I say.

"What would you call what you're doing?"

"We're walking," Ginger giggles.

"Me too!" says Chaos.

"On the sidewalk?" I point to the concrete beneath our feet.

"Ah. See you asked *what*, not where. We're doing that part differently, yes. Can I interest either of you in a cookie?" He pulls out a sandwich bag of cookies, but we shake our heads no. "Your loss. It's National Peanut Butter Cookie Day." Ginger breaks into louder giggles, but I press on with the questions.

"Why are you in the middle of the street?"

"Why not?"

"It's not safe."

"You've never been in the middle of the street before?"

Holding in a snicker, I throw my head back and ask the sky, "Why are you always like this?"

"Like what? We're all walking from here to there. I'm just doing it equidistant between the curbs, and you two are stuck in Plain Janeville, on the side of the road."

"Sidewalks are for walking!" I remind him. "On the SIDE. Of the road!"

"You do things your way and I do things my way."

"What about traffic?" I ask in a grown-up voice. He stops at this, whirls around, and snorts.

"You know what I mean," I say, chuckling.

He points to the bright yellow sign just ahead and reads it in slow motion. "Slow! Children at play."

I roll my eyes and Ginger laughs out loud.

He waves us over to the middle. "Come on, you know you wanna do it, too. Just keep your eyes and ears peeled for all the traffic"—he sweeps his arms around in a big circle—"and make a run for it if a car comes."

Ginger and I look at each other and shrug. Then we look both ways and follow him down the middle of the street.

Ginger waves her wrist toward Ms. Shae, who's still rocking glittery blue stiletto nails. She wiggles fingers at Ginger's green bracelet and cheers, "Good for you!" After the friendly chirps of the scanner, she waves Ginger on through. Then she turns to me.

I hold up my yellow bracelet, hoping no one can see my burning cheeks.

"A parent or guardian has to come when you take the deep water test," she reminds me as she runs the scanner to check me in. I muster a small smile. "Just make an appointment when you're ready. That's it, sweetie!"

She waves me on through like she didn't just embarrass me in front of everyone and turns to the next kid in line. He has a green bracelet. So do all the other kids right behind him. I hurry and catch up to Ginger, but I feel strange being the only yellow in a sea of greens.

We find chairs for our stuff when Angelica runs past and shouts, "Last one in is a rotten egg!" She soars up along with her voice, and then she plunges, *sploosh!* into the middle with her green bracelet and a big splash. Great.

Ginger runs and cannonballs right beside her. Three kids, the Jackson brothers, are already in the water and have a good laugh at all the commotion. I jump in, too, a little closer to my home base, the three-feet area. Everywhere I look, I see green bracelets. Everywhere except my own wrist. I look down at my yellow and hope all the splashes hide my shame.

"Ahh. I didn't notice earlier. I see you're a fellow member of the band!" Chaos bounces over to me. "Welcome," he says with grand flair.

"Which band?"

"The Sunshines! Those of us stuck in the shallow end." He flashes his wrist at me and I smile, glad to see I'm not the only one wearing yellow after all.

"You haven't passed the deep water test, either?" I ask.

"I haven't tried," he answers. "I can swim fine. The pool just opened like a week ago. These people are overachievers. I'll get to it. Maybe later in the summer, like National Swimming Pool Day."

"Is that a real holiday?"

"Yes, a month from now! July eleventh, to be exact."

We are interrupted by a shout of "Cannonball competition!" A kid splashes down in a perfect ball, sending water spraying and children screaming. There's a mass exodus as kids clamber out of the pool. One after another, they line up, leaping into the water, trying to make the biggest splash. *No one is jumping from the three-feet area,* I think, trying not to frown. If anyone has on a yellow besides us, I can't tell. "Let's make signs," says Chaos, elbowing my shoulder, "so we can judge next time."

I laugh, pretending to agree. But deep down, I know I'd much rather be jumping than judging. I'm just not sure when or if that'll ever happen. *You will have good luck in your personal affairs?* I guess we'll have to see.

CHAPTER 23

Dinner Date

What is that thing you have been
putting off?

Week two of soccer camp is in the books and our first exhibition match is this morning. I'm not nervous—not yet anyway. Maybe it's the music. My tablet's volume is on low, but it's loud enough for me to dance along to Flute Girl Rocks. She's doing more covers of popular songs now. Who knew "Blinding Lights" could sound so good on flute? I've added it to my list of songs to learn.

Before it's time to go, I spin the Wheel for good luck, but it lands on a question: *What is that thing you have been putting off?* I narrow my eyes at the fortune, wondering if it's some kind of joke. Mama calls me downstairs, telling me to hurry so we won't be late. I rush to eat breakfast and we head out to the field.

During the huddle before the match begins, Coach Jayme gives us last-minute directions. I can barely listen. They're really here, the coaches from the elite soccer clubs! I definitely saw someone suited up in the Charger gold and royal blue. Daddy's here, too, just like he promised.

I study the faces around the circle. Everyone is zoned in, listening to Coach, with their cheeks up. Daddy's cheeks do that, too, when his smile is ready to break free. My teammates all look excited and ready to win. Perhaps I look ready, too, but inside, butterflies are swirling. I lean into the huddle and try to pay attention.

Just before the match officially starts, Daddy's voice rings out louder than anything else, "Let's go play some footballllll!" And some of the parents on the sidelines clap and cheer. The new girls, the ones who've never met him, cringe and giggle, but I turn and blow him a big kiss and wave to Mama. It feels strange to see them standing together, like nothing has changed. I put my game face on along with everyone else and get ready to play.

After the kickoff, Wanda immediately wins the ball. I cheer her on and run. I do my best to stay locked in, watching, listening. I can actually hear when we settle into a groove. Not just because of what the parents are doing, but because the game, our movements, actually sound like music. It's percussion—swooshes, clicks, and thumps. (I can't tell Uncle J, though. He would never let me live it down.)

We lose and win the ball several times before we finally score the first goal. When it happens, everything goes in super slow motion. We all stop, mouths open, watching as the ball curves and flies past the keeper's hand. Then, normal speed, we erupt like it's the final goal of the World Cup instead of the first goal of a camp exhibition match.

It's not hot enough for water breaks, but by halftime we're all dripping with sweat.

"Everyone's doing a great job spreading the field. Keep up the good work." Coach Jayme looks over to me as I chug my second cup of water. "MJ, look around." She doesn't say any more than that, but I know what she means. I'm doing it again—hogging the ball and favoring Ginger. I nod and ready myself to do better.

My parents both wave as we head back onto the

field. In the second half, Coach subs me out a couple of times, but in the last two minutes, when the game is tied 1–1, she puts me back in and reminds me to look around. I nod, hoping the Chargers aren't making the same notes.

It's been a fast game and we're all breathing hard. When our opponents throw the ball in, I win it. Queenie and Ginger are both open. I don't know what to do. I hesitate too long, and suddenly Queenie is surrounded. I send it over to Ginger after all. She dribbles and passes to Wanda.

I try to shake it off and get back in the groove. I scan the field, looking, listening. I signal to Wanda. She passes to me and I tap it over to Angelica, who *BOOM*, launches it pistol-straight and GOOOOAAALLLL!! The whistle blows, 2–1 us. It's over! After a cheerful celebration on the field and a huge congratulations from Coach, we all run our separate ways.

"Be right back!" I yell to Ginger. We're riding with her for ice cream this time, as soon as we say goodbye to our parents.

"You played so great, Babygirl! Congrats on that assist." Daddy throws his arms out wide and I run into them, wishing I could stay there all afternoon.

"You think the Chargers noticed?"

"Of course they did!"

"So, we were thinking . . . ," says Mama, "what about a celebration dinner with Daddy?"

"Are you kidding? It's Friday, too! We can even play Clue again instead of—"

"Well, that's not quite what we meant." I freeze while they look at each other as if deciding who will explain. My stomach churns into a knot.

"MJ, we were thinking you can spend the day with me," says Daddy, trying to sound cheerful. "After y'all get your ice cream, I can pick you up. We can hang out for the afternoon and I'll cook some of your favorites for dinner tonight."

"No!" It escapes from my mouth before I even realize what's happening. I don't mean to say it so fast, but Daddy's face is just as quick. His lips draw tight, and I immediately wish I could take it back. At the same time, going to *his* place is not what I pictured at all. I want Daddy at home. His real home.

"Daddy, I don't want to go see you in some strange place."

"It's not strange, MJ. I live there," he says quietly.

"No, you're just there for now!" The heat that usually shows up only for Mama is here for them both. "You're 'trying it out.' But it doesn't fit."

"It's tough for us all, MJ. But this is just the way it is for another few weeks. You can come over today, or we can try another time."

I feel bad for losing my temper. I melt back into him, apologizing with a hug. I don't want to hurt his feelings, but there's no way I can say yes. I can't see myself there. Not yet. This morning's fortune asked, *What is that thing you have been putting off?* This. Definitely this. I exhale and say quietly into his chest, "No, Daddy. Not today."

He nods and we kiss nose-to-nose. I turn away as fast as I can, before the tears show up. Across the parking lot, I catch Ginger staring, waiting on me for ice cream. I duck into Mama's car, bury my face in my hands, and cry.

⭐

CHAPTER 24

Disappearing Act

Now is the best time for you to be
spontaneous. Serendipity!

Mama is quiet the whole way home. As soon as we get inside, she tries to tell me something, but I block it out. Whatever it is, I don't wanna hear it. I don't wanna hear anything. We won! I played well! Mostly. And then they go and ruin it, trying to make me see "Daddy's place."

This is Daddy's place.

I take a shower, change clothes, and hide out in my room.

"Maya!" Mama's voice is close, but I don't answer.

"I have a donors' luncheon starting soon. Do you want to come?" she asks, opening my door. I shake my head. I never go with her to those things.

"I know you must be disappointed Daddy's not having dinner here tonight. Are you ready to talk about it?"

I shake my head again, refusing to look at her. She sighs.

"I won't be gone long. I just have to smile and wave. There's leftovers in the fridge you can heat up for lunch. Okay?"

I nod this time.

She hesitates in the doorway. I know she is waiting on me to say something, but I get my stubbornness from her. I feel her shifting, like she wants to come closer to me. I tighten my body, willing her to stay away. I just want her to leave. Me. Alone.

When she finally says goodbye, there are no smiles. No exclamation points of forced excitement—*bangs* as Daddy calls them. Just another sigh. I hear the stillness settle over the house when she leaves.

I grab Flicker and dig out a folder of old sheet music from when I first learned to play real songs. I try "Air for Winds," playing out loud for the first time in ages. I loved playing this song with the other kids. It felt so satisfying the way the notes landed right in the middle of my chest when we all played in tune. I even used to record myself practicing, just so I could play along and harmonize.

I hold the last note as long as I can. When I finally inhale again, I am staring at the deep blue paint on the Wheel. This has to end, this trial separation. I know it's only six more weeks, but what if they decide to do it forever?

I walk over to the Wheel and spin, hoping for a hint about what to do next. I close my eyes and and await the verdict.

Now is the best time for you to be spontaneous. Serendipity!

I can be spontaneous. What if I disappear for a while? They will be upset if I'm gone. They will be sorry they put me through this. I don't have to go very far or for very long . . . maybe just a day or so. Long enough to make them worry, to show them this trial is a horrible idea.

I gather all of my cash, about twelve dollars; my tablet, in case I need to send a message or call; and one outfit, and stuff it all in my soccer bag. I run downstairs to grab some snacks—a bag of popcorn and a banana. I have no idea where I'm going, but it will be away from here.

"What are you doing?" I ask Chaos. He is lying on his back in his front yard, and I can't resist stopping. I still haven't decided exactly where I'm going, so maybe he can help me improvise some ideas.

"I am naming the clouds. That one"—he points to one resembling a horse—"is called Susan."

"Susan?"

"Yep. You try. It's a cloud. You can name it anything you want." He sounds quite sure of himself, like there's nothing at all strange about what he's doing. I plop down beside him, but I am iffy about this game.

"I feel silly naming a cloud," I say. "I mean, that's clearly a horse. But why would I call it *Susan*?"

"You're willing to call it a *horse*, but not *Susan*? I don't see the horse. But I definitely see Susan."

"I guess when I name something, I expect it to be around for a while. These clouds are rolling away."

"So?"

We sit silently until he points to another cloud. "That's Jack," he announces.

"The heart?"

"You say *heart*. I say *Jack*."

"Whoever heard of a heart named Jack?"

"You've never played solitaire? You know—Jack. Of Hearts?"

"This is a little strange, Chaos."

"You're the strange one," he says, still staring at the sky.

"Me?"

"Well, you have a soccer bag, and the soccer field isn't in walking distance. But you're not really dressed for the pool. Ginger's house is that way and you were going this way. So you're going somewhere. You're stopping to name clouds, so you're not in a hurry. Seems strange to me."

"Oh." More silence. "I'm playing a game."

He looks at me and squints.

I pretend not to notice him looking and stare up at the clouds. "I'm playing hide-and-seek," I say. "Oh, look—there's a hand! See the fingers all spread out?"

"With a bag? Isn't that called 'running away'? Won't your parents worry? And on International Panic Day, at that."

Silence again. "Parent," I say finally. "Maybe."

"I thought you lived with both of your parents. I

139

just saw them at the cookout."

I continue to study the clouds, but really, I am deciding how much I will share. Chaos waits quietly. Which I guess is easy to do since he was by himself before I came along.

"They're doing some kind of 'trial separation.' And they're acting like it's normal and . . . it's not. Anyway, I'm being spontaneous."

"They're probably upset, too. I think grown-ups just hide it better. There's Robert."

I shake my head at Robert.

"My mom calls it putting on a brave face," he continues.

"I don't want brave faces. I want my daddy at home."

"You're looking at this the wrong way."

"There's no other way to look at your family falling apart. There's no bright side!"

"Yeah, it sucks, but you can still look at it another way. Like that Jacqueline rolling by. One second." He holds up a hand like he needs time for something. He closes his eyes and hums.

"What are you doing?"

"Thinking," he says, his eyes still closed.

"Thinking?"

"Shh. Yes."

"But you're humming a song."

"Shh."

"Wait. Is that the *Jeopardy!* theme song? Why are you doing that?"

He opens his eyes super wide and shouts, "IT HELPS ME THINK. But not when people are interrupting! Okay, the category is *Laws*."

"What?"

"Ask me the answer."

"This is not how you play *Jeopardy!*"

"Please just ask!"

"Ugh. What's the answer?"

"*Law of Conservation*. Tell me the question."

"What is *Energy cannot be created nor destroyed*?"

"Exactly. Like love. It's a type of energy, right? I think family is energy, too. Your family is not destroyed. It's just changing forms. Your dad is still your dad. I'm guessing he loves you the same. It just looks different because he's not there."

"No. That doesn't work. My family didn't exist before. Then it was created when my parents got together and had me. And now it's destroyed. DEstroyed!"

"Well, what's gonna happen if you leave, too?"

"I was only leaving for a little while," I say to the grass. I steal a glance toward my house. Mama will be home from her luncheon soon, wondering where I went.

"I need a name for that one." He points.

I look up. "The sailboat?"

"Yup."

"I don't know," I say, standing up and pulling on my bag. "Bob."

"That's a great name for that cloud. Good luck with the hide-and-seek game. Hope you find what you're looking for."

I almost correct him and remind him that I'm not looking for anything. But then I think, maybe he's right. I *am* looking for something.

Happiness.

CHAPTER 25

☆

Happily Ever After

You will have good luck and overcome many hardships.

I leave Chaos and go straight to Ginger's. I want to tell her the truth. I can't put it off any longer. But when I arrive, I stand there, waiting, as if someone will just fling open the door. No one does. Still, I can't bring myself to ring the bell. Instead, I stare at the peephole, feeling silly.

I turn around and look up at the clouds. I think about the one named Bob, and Chaos telling me he hopes I find what I'm looking for. Me too. Deep down, I'm afraid that once I tell Ginger about Daddy, it will be true. Really true. My parents will be separated, maybe even forever. Even though I'm scared to tell her, real friends don't keep secrets from each other. From being jealous about the Golden Astro to never telling her about my parents, I haven't been a real friend in forever.

I take a deep breath, gather all my courage, and raise my finger to the bell. But before I press it, the door swings open. Ginger is standing there shining like the sun.

She screams—a happy, laughing scream. "Hey!" She yells as she waves me in.

"Hurry up!" She skips away and I follow her to her room.

When we get to the door, she stands to the side so I can go in first. I gasp. Instead of the baby blue and white room with twin beds that I'm used to, I walk into a lemony-yellow wonderland with bunk beds. It's beautiful, but I'm shocked. Disappointed. She didn't even send me a picture or anything. Real best friends would never change their whole room without saying a word. The list of things we haven't told each other just keeps growing. She watches me eyeing everything.

"You like it?" she belts, bright and cheerful, like it hadn't crossed her mind my feelings might be hurt.

"Yeah. It's great." I try to sound happy for her, but

here I am, for the second time, barely able to muster a real smile when she has good news. "I'm just . . . surprised to see it."

"Me too!"

"Huh?"

"My mom said she wanted to cheer me up, so she surprised me by redoing my room while I stayed with my aunt. I was just about to come get you and there you were!" Her huge smile seems so genuine, but it doesn't ease the tightness in my heart.

"I don't believe it."

"Why?" Confusion clouds her face.

"I thought . . . maybe you had a new best friend."

"Who?"

"Angelica."

"Oh! No . . ." She looks away, and her cheeks flush. Again. I wait to see if she'll explain.

"It's not like that. You're still my best friend. There's just. Lots of stuff."

I toss my soccer bag to the floor and sit on the lower bunk. She plops down in front of me.

"We missed you for ice cream," she says, changing the subject.

Now it's my turn to have a red face.

"Did you get in trouble?"

"No. Something happened," I admit, "but I'm not in trouble."

She waits for me to keep going, but I can't bring myself to say more. Not yet.

"I have something to tell you," she says softly. One look at her face, and I know it's important. Really important.

"I'm ready." I scoot off the bed and onto the floor with her. She presses her knees against mine, like we always do when we're sharing our Deep Downs.

I lean in to listen. She's quiet a long time.

"Pa Pa forgot me." Her voice breaks, like the low notes of a sad song. I draw in a sharp breath and wait.

"A few weeks ago we went to visit him, and he asked my mom who I was. 'And who's that pretty young lady?'" She points, imitating him.

"Ginger!" I whisper, shocked.

"I know he hasn't been feeling good, but my own grandpa forgot me."

"I'm sorry." I grab her hands and squeeze. She squeezes back. "What can you do?"

"Nothing. They say we just have to prepare ourselves that things like this will happen more often and last longer. That's why sometimes I don't ride with you as much. We've been spending more time with him, and we just never know when he might . . . forget things."

I think back to the banquet. She said she'd see me there. And he was there, too. He looked fine then.

"The day he forgot me, it was just for a few minutes and he seemed to remember me after a while. But . . . ," she whispers, "I never thought he could forget me. Look."

She shows me a collage of pictures of the two of them. I know a lot of those moments. I am there, not in the picture but in the room, for almost every single one.

"This is why you wanted these pictures from my house?"

"Yeah. I want to give him this to help him remember."

I nod, not knowing what else to say. Pa Pa is always so sparkly. I hate to think of him losing his memory.

"I wanted to tell you," she says. "There just hasn't been a good time."

I think back to the rainy-day tackle, when I was really down and I saw her sadness, too. I had been so caught up in my own world, I didn't even ask about hers. No wonder she's talking to Angelica.

We're silent again. I inhale as much air as I can, then blow it all out.

"You know what I want this summer?" I ask.

"To become a Charger?"

She's right, of course, but it sounds funny. Like the wrong note in the middle of a song, or an instrument out of tune.

"Sort of. But not for me."

"Who?"

"Daddy."

"True! You know he would eat that up!"

"Yeah."

"Well. What do *you* want?"

"Happily ever after."

"Like in the movies? When everything works out the way it's supposed to?"

I nod, put my head on my knees, and cry. Ginger grabs my hand then and squeezes it, waiting. I squeeze back.

"Daddy left. Well, I think Mama asked him to leave. I don't know. They are doing a 'trial separation' to see . . ." I stop midsentence before I burst into tears again.

I peer at Ginger, into her big, round eyes. She looks like she just saw the monster in a horror movie. She grabs both hands now. Holding them tight. When I get myself together enough, I try again.

"They are separated for now to see if they like it. But *I* don't like it. So this summer I want us to be happy all together again."

She looks at me, almost through me, and I wonder if she is thinking about herself. About what she would do if her daddy left.

"What are you gonna do?"

"What *can* I do?"

"Well, I don't know about happily ever after, but me and you can be happy today." She jumps up and reaches out a hand to me. "Let's go to the pool!"

"I have to go home and get my suit." Mama's definitely back by now. *Guess this means I'm not running away.* I smile to myself.

"You have one here from last summer! It still fits, right?"

She tosses me a red swimsuit. I get dressed as fast as I can. She hands me a towel, and off we go.

"It's after three! If we hurry, we'll be there in time for cannonballs and Marco! Ohh," she says, eyeing my wrist, "we have to stop by your house and get your bracelet first, though."

Oh right, I think. *The yellow one.*

CHAPTER 26

Meet the Champ

You will discover an unexpected
treasure.

After an hour at the pool, I tell Ginger it's time
for me to get back home. The truth is, I'm tired
of feeling embarrassed. No matter what Chaos said
before about the Sunshines, I'm the only one with a
yellow bracelet still. Even he had a green today. The
whole neighborhood was there for Marco Madness.
It's not just cannonballs and Marco Polo now. It's
Sharks and Minnows, water volleyball, whatever you
can think of. In the late afternoon, everybody's there
and everybody's green.

Everybody except me.

150

On the soccer field, I can run from one end to the other. The only thing that can hold me back is an opponent, but I always find a way around them. I look for the openings and go. But the pool is different. I don't want to be trapped at the shallow end all summer because of a bracelet. Or . . . because I'm too scared to master the deep. I want to be free to go wherever, whenever. I want to yell "Marco" one day.

Mama raises her eyebrows when she sees me back home so early, but she doesn't ask why, and I don't explain. Up in my room, I turn out all of my drawers, searching for my goggles. I thought there was a kickboard somewhere, too. Anything that can help me learn to swim.

I plop down on a pile of everything and try to picture where more pool stuff would be. Maybe one of those storage boxes in the closet. Mama and Daddy's closet. I sigh thinking about going in there again, but that's the best next place to look. I tiptoe to their room to go see.

I force myself to ignore the bin of Daddy's T-shirts. I really wanna dig in it, to pick out another shirt and see if I can smell his scent, but I don't. Instead I open a different bin, but it looks like sweaters and random stuff. Nothing that seems related to summer.

There's only one more left, but just as I'm about to open it, I spy a box on the top shelf. A hatbox like the kind Grandma has for her wigs. I've never seen Mama in a wig. I snatch down the square black box, smiling, wondering what kind of wig I'll find. I remove the lid slowly, trying to sneak a peek and surprise myself at the same time, but all I can see in the shadows is more black. I reach in and my hand brushes against a stiff velvet cloth. "Eww!" My skin crawls. I can't stand the feel of thick velvet. Suddenly the hairs stand up on my arm. Something hard is underneath. *I know what this is!*

I yank the black velvet away and there it is. The photo album Uncle J told me about. It's green, alright. But not the dark green I expected.

Lime green?

I sit on the floor with my legs crossed and pull it onto my lap. I open to the first page, taking my time, and when it finally lies flat, my mouth drops to the floor. Mama!

She looks almost the same, except she is so . . . smiley. Like I can barely see the rest of her face because of her enormous smile. Before she dimmed, she gave beautiful light beams of smiles, but nothing quite as bright as this. Same short hair, but it's closer to blond than the dark brown it is now. She is laughing. Even her eyes are smiling, like whatever was making her laugh started from somewhere deep inside and exploded in a big whoosh of joy.

I flip through the album. There's Daddy. Loud and laughing, even in a photo. They're so young. *They look like models.* I continue to flip, stepping through a life I can't imagine even though it's right there in my lap. Once in a while, Daddy and Uncle Jimmy. Mama and Daddy. The three of them. An unidentified woman made it a double date. They were at parties, on the yard at Florida A&M University – FAMU, in classrooms, everywhere. *Flip, flip, flip.*

Daddy and Mama selling baked goods at the swap meet on campus. And then something totally different: a photo of a pool, and women lined up ready to jump in. A race. Another shot and they are in the air—diving into the water with their hands pointed like arrows. A picture of a woman in a dark green and orange swimsuit, studying the scoreboard, punching the air. This one is glossy and sharp, like a professional took it. The next one is a close-up of the scoreboard. Anderson. *Mama's maiden name!*

I flip again, and there she is, smiling that huge explosion of a smile. One that looks so familiar in these pictures but like nothing that I've seen lately. I keep flipping, page after page of her in that dark green FAMU swimsuit. On the podium. Waving ribbons and chomping medals. She won! A lot! A few more pictures of Mama and Daddy together. And then a blank page at the end. I close the album and sit for a second.

Mama really *is* a swimmer. A champion swimmer!

⭐

CHAPTER 27

When the Student Is Ready

A new relationship is about to blossom. You will be blessed.

"**M**ama." It comes out just above a whisper. I feel almost nervous for some reason. She doesn't turn around at first, so I call out to her again.

"Mama!" I'm loud enough now, and my lingering shock feels like anger. She swivels in the chair and the late afternoon's fading sunlight falls across her face. Her eyes are questioning, wondering what's on my mind, but before she says anything, she spots the lime-green book.

"Where did you find that?"

"Is this you?" I flip to a picture and point. Her smile is the biggest thing on the page. She is tiny and curvy in her deep-green swimsuit. A gold medal hangs around her neck.

"Don't sound so surprised. I have the same hairstyle and everything." Her mouth creeps into a smile.

I study her low cut. She's right, of course.

"But you look. Different." I don't wanna say *happier*, but that's what it is. Everything else about her is the same, even after all this time. It's just that smile. It's deep down. From her toes.

"I don't look that different, do I?" She fingers her spiky hair as she flips through pages from the beginning, smiling, sighing. Her face gets darker the closer she gets to the end. I almost think she's forgotten I'm here until she speaks again.

"Yep, it's me. And your daddy, and Uncle Jimmy. They called us *the triplets*."

"You swam in college?" It's obvious at this point, but still incredible to believe. Why has no one ever told me? Uncle J said Mama lived in the water when they were young, but it's hard to imagine parents *before* they were parents. A whole lifetime ago.

"I told you I could! Full scholarship. Swam all four years. Well, almost all. Missed a few meets senior year.

Best time of my life!" She says it so strong and proud. A real *bang* at the end. The way Daddy sounds when he talks about soccer. The woman sitting in front of me is my mother, but I'm meeting her for the first time.

"Why don't you swim now? I mean, why did you stop?"

She shrugs and starts to look more like herself—the person I know best these days, anyway. It's like watching the sun set, the way her smile recedes until it disappears completely.

She flips a few pages in the book, and stops at a picture of herself laughing in the water. She stares at it and then rubs it, almost as if she's smoothing the page.

"You know who this is a picture of?"

"Um. It's you."

"It's me, yes. But it's you, too. I didn't know it then, but . . . you were already on the way. A few months after this picture, I stopped swimming."

"Forever?"

"Well. There's a lot more to it. But yes, there came a time when I didn't want to see or even be anywhere near a pool again. I didn't even want to hear the word." She sets her jaw, but I can't really read her face. Is it angry? Sad? I stand there, staring, and wondering what the "more to it" is. I add it to my list of questions that I don't ask out loud.

"So, you'll get in a pool now?"

"For you? Yes. For you and for me, too. It's time," she says softly. She inhales and claps her hands together. "So . . . the secret is out. Do you want to pass that deep water test or no?"

Before I answer, she opens the album from the beginning once more. I slip away to my room. Yes, I do want to pass that deep water test. I just don't know if Mama's the one to help me. I still think it's her fault that Daddy left. I still haven't forgiven her for that.

Maybe I'll spin my Wheel of Fortunes and see what comes up.

CHAPTER 28

Father's Day

**Tomorrow is a good day for trying
something new.**

"Are you coming inside?" I ask Mama as she pulls into the apartment complex. She's wearing big shades that cover half her face, but the bright yellow frames seem way too cheerful for what we're up to. Even the buildings are bland—brown slats with brown stones. Daddy is inside one of them.

"No," she says, and the word lingers in the air, as if other words are not far behind. But if they are, she doesn't say them.

"Don't you wanna see it?"

She sighs, but doesn't answer. I take that as a yes

but no, because that's how I feel, too. She walks me to the door of Daddy's place.

Daddy's place.

I hate, hate, hate thinking of it that way. It's Father's Day, so everyone thought today was the best day for me to finally come. I've brought a gift—Jenga—and a card.

She nods at me to ring the bell. It feels so strange, ringing the bell to see him. He opens the door, all smiles. "There's my girl!" he shouts, big and loud as if nothing has changed. "Nice shades, Leah." She half smiles and nods at this.

"I'll bring her back later on," he says.

Mama waves, turning away quickly. "Be good, Maya. I'll see y'all later."

And just like that, she is in the car and driving away. I don't like watching her leave without us any more than I liked it when Daddy did it.

Maybe he's thinking what I'm thinking, because he sighs. He squeezes my shoulder and asks, "Are those for me?" I look up at him and nod, and we go inside.

"I got you a copy of the key," he says. "That way you don't have to ring the bell. This is your place, too." I ball my fist at that. My place is his place is Mama's place, and it is five minutes away from whatever this place is.

He takes me on a tour. It's nice, although everything is white and gray and dark brown. There is one bedroom, and the gray furniture and white dishes came with the apartment. Good. It will be easy for him to move right back home at the end of summer.

When we return to the living room, I smile when I see he's brought Bananagrams and Mancala. These are his favorites, not mine, but I'm glad they're here.

"You can bring *your* favorites next time," he says. We lock eyes and laugh.

We don't go outside, but I do wonder if there's a grill somewhere nearby. There's still plenty of time left in the summer, and I know the Grill Master will not be satisfied cooking indoors all the time. He turns on the television, and it's already tuned to the Afro Cuban Jazz station. Just like at home. The real one.

"Hungry?" he asks.

"Yes!"

"Brunch first, and then I'll open my gift. How's that?"

The thought of his cooking brings a real smile to

my face. He waves me closer, dancing to "Michaela" by Sonora Carruseles. This was one of Mama's favorite songs, once upon a time. I smile at the memory of her smooth spins and shines. My mouth waters as he pulls out eggs and grits and oysters and gets to work.

After a while, I venture around again. He's done a few things to make it homey, like lay pictures of our family on the living room table. I pick one up and stare at myself. It's from the first day of school this past year. I am grinning, standing with one foot on my electric-blue soccer ball. My parents are still together, and I am full of hope for a great year of soccer.

That was all Before. At some point between then and now, my parents had secret talks about splitting up and tried to disappear me so I wouldn't even know. As for soccer . . .

I look over at him cooking and humming and having fun, and suddenly I get prickly. Why is he dancing around in this gray kitchen? Why isn't he home in *our* kitchen dancing around? The more I watch him, the hotter I get.

"Your face is mighty wrinkly," he says, eyeing me. "Whatcha thinking about?"

"How come you're dancing?"

"What do you mean?"

"You're dancing! You're smiling like everything's fine. It's not fine!" I flop down in a chair, arms folded across my chest.

"I don't like being away from you or your mom even for one second."

"Well, come back!"

"It's not that simple. Your mom and I agreed."

"*I* didn't agree," I say to the gray carpet. "Nobody asked me."

"That's fair. Let's talk about it. What's on your mind? You can ask me anything."

Why did you agree to leave? How will you know if the trial separation worked? What's the exact date you're coming back home? More questions for my long list, but none I really want to ask out loud yet.

"I just think you should come back."

"A setback is just a setup for a what?" He points at me.

"Daddy. A comeback."

"It's a setback. Your mom and I have been together for a long time. Since high school. Don't look at it like it's the end of the game—it's more like halftime or a water break."

"Doesn't taste like water to me. More like poison." I cough and hack and pretend to gag.

"Poison? Yikes. That's pretty dramatic. I'll tell you what. Let's change this poison into medicine."

"What does that mean?"

"It means you can still make something good from all of this. We had a lot of time together because of our soccer Saturdays. Now you have more time with your mom."

"You sound like Uncle J."

"He'll never be Grill Master, but he does get some things right." I shake my head as he begins to dredge oysters through a mixture of seasoned flour and corn-meal.

"She wants to help me pass the deep water test."

"So I've heard." He smiles. "Leah the mermaid."

"How come everyone knows that but me?"

"Well, now you get to find out, right?"

"I guess."

When I spun the Wheel this morning, it said, *Tomorrow is a good day for trying something new.* I'm still not sure learning to swim with Mama is a great idea, but perhaps the Wheel knows something I don't. Maybe I'll try it. For Daddy.

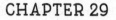

CHAPTER 29

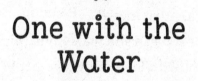

One with the Water

You will soon receive an unusual gift.

Mama and I walk to the pool for our first lesson. I don't have much to say because the butterflies in my stomach are doing all the talking. With every step, I tug my yellow bracelet to calm them down. It's not working. What if she gets impatient? We have the same short temper, and on top of that, I *want* to be mad at her. This could be a disaster. On the other hand, deep down, I can't wait to see her swim.

I steal a look at her, at the sun dancing on her brown cheeks. She looks radiant and relaxed, but leaning forward at the same time. Almost as if she wants to run to the pool like a little kid on their way to go do something fun. Come to think of it, Angelica looks that way before games. Leaning. Ready to go. I wonder if I lean forward on my way to the field. I'll have to pay attention next time.

It's early and no one else is here yet, just like Ginger said. I'm glad. I wouldn't want the whole neighborhood watching us. Especially not this first time. We do some light stretches in the pool to begin. Then we practice blowing bubbles and kicking. I mostly know how to do it, but Mama says I need to really master them, just like my touches. Next, we try back float. I stretch out, ears underwater, back arched like she tells me to. Her voice is muffled by the water, but I can hear her telling me to relax and keep breathing.

"There you go," she says. The tender smile in her voice invites a tiny smile from my lips. My anger is still in here somewhere, but it's hard to keep it close. *This is kinda fun so far,* I admit to myself.

"You try that for a few minutes or practice your bubbles and kicks. I'll be back."

"Where are you going?" I call out, although she is already moving away.

"Just down and back. Keep floating." And for a

few seconds, I do. But I want to watch. I bring my knees to my chest and stand up just as she starts.

She slides through the water with barely a splash, and makes her way down nearly half the pool before resurfacing. When she reaches the deep end, she flip turns and cuts through the water. Huge drops fly and she speeds up as she approaches my end. When she arrives, she touches the wall and comes up for air, breathing hard but laughing. Laughing! My stingy smile relaxes.

"Whew! I'm out of shape! And you're supposed to be practicing!" She giggles, but she wastes no time starting down again. I lean back, ears under, back arched once more. I feel the ripples as she slides through the water, getting far away before she kicks. I am still floating when she returns this time, but when she goes back down, I watch.

Mama is one with the water. Again she glides. She really is a mermaid. A dolphin. A ballerina, dancing in water. When she reaches the other end this time, she stops at the wall and throws her head back to the sun. She looks like the girl in the photo album, happy and at peace. This morning's fortune on the Wheel said, *You will soon receive an unusual gift.* I wonder if this is it. Seeing her at peace.

Why doesn't she look like that all the time? Is it Daddy's fault? Is that why she wanted him to leave?

She heads this way again, with her powerful kicks and strokes. In no time at all, she's back to me. She stands up, brushing the water off her face, laughing still. I want to snuggle up to her. To be closer to this sweet, smiling version of Mama. I've missed her. Why can't I have them both, Mama and Daddy, smiling together? They smiled together before. Can't they do it again?

"Why are you so frowny?" she asks, her face clouding over.

"I was just watching."

"Ready?"

"To do that?" My bubbles and kicks could never possibly be anything like that majesty.

"Well, no, not yet, silly." She laughs. "But we all have to start somewhere. Let's see what you can do."

I shake off my thoughts of a happy family and push off the wall with arrow-shaped hands. It feels funny, but I think I'm doing it right. After I show her a few times, she nods her approval.

"These are the basics, Babygirl. Once you have these down, we'll be ready to add on." A jolt flies through me at "Babygirl." A quick flash of heat rising. I'm having a good time, but I don't wanna hear that from her, not even with a big smile on her face. I don't wanna hear that from anyone but Daddy.

CHAPTER 30

⭐

The Deep Downs

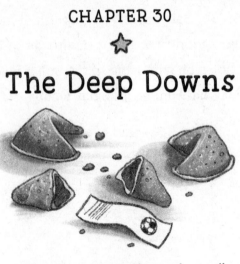

Someone in your life needs a call
from you.

When we get back home, I change clothes and video-call Ginger, but she doesn't answer. I pull out Flicker and play the scales so I don't have to concentrate on what I'm doing. Instead, I can think about me and Mama in the pool. I've never seen anyone swim that way before. She said there was a time she didn't even want to hear the word *pool*. Sometime after I was born.

I hope she didn't stop because of me.

Ginger videos me back, and her face is really close to the screen. So close, I can count her freckles.

"Hey! Pa Pa loves it!" she whisper-shouts.

"The collage?"

"Yes! He wants to make one, too! He says he has lots of pictures of me, so when I come back, I can help him put it together."

"What made you think to do a collage?"

She pauses, as if the question caught her off guard. "Angelica."

"Oh."

We're both quiet a minute, but then she whispers again. "Her aunt has dementia. Angelica and her mom made a scrapbook of things they wanted her to remember. I decided to try it, too."

I nod but don't say anything.

"Why don't you like her anymore?"

"I like her. . . . It just seemed like you were talking to her all the time. Without me."

"Oh. It's because I remembered hearing about her aunt, so I asked about it. We just talk about, what it's like, you know."

"Oh."

"Angelica's cool. And she loves playing soccer with you."

I love every minute! she'd said.

"Well, why is she always yelling at me?"

171

"What do you mean?"

"She's always like, 'Such and such is open, MJ!'"

"Oh, girl. She just wants to elevate your game! But enough about soccer. Tell me about today!" She leans forward into the screen again and whispers, "How did it go with your mom?"

"I don't know."

"What do you mean?"

"I mean . . . I don't know." I lower my voice and lean forward, too. "I'm mad at her. For. You know."

Ginger nods.

"But she was totally different in the water," I whisper.

"Different how?" Her eyes widen and her eyebrows go all the way up. I blink, picturing Mama's smile. Her big laugh as she threw her head back to the sun. Her peace.

"She was happy."

"So why are you looking mad now?"

"I'm not mad. I'm . . . confused. I just don't get it."

"Get what?"

"It's just, everything is different now. I don't know—"

"Oh wait. That's Pa Pa. Sorry! Gotta go!"

Ginger ends the call, and I study the screen where

her freckles used to be. Mama was totally different in the water. She smiled a real smile. The thing I've wanted to see all this time was right there. Now I just don't know how to feel about it all.

I go to the Wheel for advice. What does it all mean? What should I do? I spin, spin, spin and watch as it comes to a stop. It finally lands on: *Someone in your life needs a call from you.*

I just talked to Ginger. There's only one other person I'd call right now. Daddy. But I really have no idea how to tell him everything on my mind. I plop back into the Cave, scrolling through videos on Flute Girl Rocks, thinking about what to say. But after a few minutes, it's time to quit stalling. I press the button to video-call him. He answers with a huge smile.

"MJ!"

"Hi, Daddy."

"Uh-oh. What's wrong?"

"You promise not to laugh?"

"Of course. What's up?"

I stare at the worry wrinkles in his forehead. I rub my own forehead in case mine is wrinkled, too. He watches me and waits.

"We went swimming today."

"That's right! How'd it go?" He settles in with a hopeful smile, but I don't give him one back.

"She can really swim."

"Yeah? What else?"

"I saw her smile. Her real one."

"I see."

I take a deep breath, still trying to figure out the best way to ask what I want to know. I don't wanna hurt Daddy's feelings. But I do wanna know why she could smile so big—without him. Finally, I blurt it out.

"Was she smiling because she was in the pool? Or because she was in the pool and . . . you weren't with us? No laughing—you promised." His face grows serious again.

"I'm not laughing. That's a pretty heavy question." He rubs his hand over his bald head, staring off for a little while, thinking.

"I thought it was Mama's fault that you left. But now I don't know what to think. She smiled, just like she did in that bright green book."

"The photo album?" His face softens. I nod.

"I'll bet she lit up the whole pool," he says, smiling now. I nod again.

"She did! It was . . ." I don't want to say it was weird, but in a way it was. "Have you noticed she doesn't smile as much as she used to? And I never see her smile like that at soccer games. Or anytime you bring up soccer, really. Especially club soccer."

"Well, soccer is *our* thing."

My stomach lurches a little when he says that, but I ignore it.

"Swimming was her thing," I say. "But she stopped swimming after she had me."

"That's not your fault, if that's what you're thinking. It's complicated. A lot of things happened that neither of us wanted to talk about. But maybe now it's time. It's not good to keep the truth bottled up inside."

"Me and Ginger call it our Deep Downs."

"Deep Downs?"

"Yeah. It's the stuff we don't really wanna tell anybody. But sometimes we tell each other."

"I like that," he says, nodding. "Yeah, we need to be better at sharing our Deep Downs. All three of us."

"Daddy?"

"Yes?"

"How much longer is the trial separation? Is it really five weeks? Five weeks and two days?"

"Deep Down?"

I nod.

"I'm not sure, Babygirl. We'll see."

CHAPTER 31

☆

A New Groove

When there is something you
enjoy, do more of it.

"Last one. Go!"

Coach Jayme yells and blows the whistle to start the clock on today's final drill. Forty-five minutes of torture, almost over. There are three teams: five players per team, five minutes per game. The winner stays on the field and faces the new team. After eight rounds I'm beat, but there's just one more to play. One more until I can go home and relax with Flicker.

"Whoops!" I yell after I kick the ball to Ginger. I don't go straight to her every time, but it still happens more than it should. Old habits die hard.

"Recover!" yells Angelica, apparently trying to elevate my game.

I roll my eyes, but I run into position when the ball comes back my way. I scan the field. Erica's open. I don't usually pass to her for goals because of her "all left, all the time" thing. This summer she decided she wanted to develop her left foot, so whenever she can, she uses it. She misses, every time. But she's ready, so I launch it over to her. She dribbles and GOALLLL! Her first one all summer.

We erupt, screaming. Even the campers on the sidelines join in.

"Keep moving!" Coach yells, but we can't help it.

"Coach, that was greatness, admit it!" I yell, running past her. She laughs and calls out, "Yes, it was. Now get back in the zone. One minute left!" The big closing exhibition is just a week away, and Coach says every second is crucial. Finally, *finally*, she blows the whistle when time is up.

Uncle J is here to scoop me. I walk full speed ahead toward his Jeep with all the energy I have left. Playing soccer three hours a day in the Georgia summer is super hard. The other girls are chugging water or lying out in the grass, in no hurry to leave. Not me. It's fun to kick the ball around, to dance with my teammates as we move up and down the field. And it's satisfying when the ball whooshes into the net. But when time is up, I'm ready to go.

Flicker is different. I *always* want to play and get lost in the music, where time disappears. I love when my fingers dance on the keys during fast songs. Today there's a new song I want to practice. Flute Girl is learning "Flight of the Bumblebee." That's way too hard for me right now, but that's okay. I will practice every day until it's a part of me.

"You down for the park?" Uncle J asks as I hop in.

"Sure!"

"What about your friends?" He nods to Ginger and Angelica, who are waving goodbye.

"They're busy. They're working on something."

"Without you?" he says, his eyebrows up.

I nod.

"And that's okay?"

"Yeah. Everything is okay. I've been listening"—I tug my earlobe—"and we are all hearing each other just fine."

"Nice! Let's get some lunch and clean clothes and head out. The flute choir is playing this afternoon."

"What?" I clap. "I LOVE THE FLUTE CHOIR!"

"And that's why I'm your number one uncle."

I roll my eyes. "You're my only uncle."

"That sounds like number one to me."

"How's it been?" Uncle J asks about camp as we set up at the park. "Better? Having any fun yet?"

"Better, yeah," I tell him. "We all click now and I'm trying new moves. It's nice when things all just fit together. Feels like . . ."

"Jazz?"

I grunt. "I guess. I can't wait for the exhibition."

"So you're playing well and the team is gelling—but are you having fun? You didn't answer that part."

"It's fine."

"Fun, MJ. You're still a kid. You know what fun is, don't you?"

"Uncle!" Fun is when you smile real smiles and laugh out loud. Like Mama in the water. I have a good time at camp, I really do. But . . .

I love every minute! Maybe not as much fun as Angelica.

"Soccer's fine."

"I dig it." He throws both hands up in defeat. "If you need something to do when camp ends, I can get you back up to speed on your flute."

There it is. Another chance to tell him the truth, that I've been playing all along. That I miss playing out loud, and that I would love to play with him any day.

But I chose soccer. Daddy and I spent hours on soccer this year because that's what I picked. I can't look like I'm backing down now, not this close to club tryouts. How would that make Daddy feel? Plus, telling the truth about Flicker to Uncle J or anyone might jinx my chances with the Chargers. I don't need any more bad luck.

"What makes you think I wanna go back to my flute?" I say, trying to sound surprised by the suggestion.

He stares at me like my nose is on backward.

I touch it just to be sure. "What?"

"I thought you just said you've been listening better. Have you been listening to *yourself*, too?"

"What are you talking about?"

"Me earlier." He points to himself. "'The flute choir is playing today.' You . . ." He points at me, then claps his hands together in delight. "'What?'" he says in a high voice. "'I LOVE THE FLUTE CHOIR!'"

I throw my head back in protest. "Ugh! I did not do all that."

"Yes, yes you did. 'Whaaat? I LUUUVVV the flute choir!'"

I suck my teeth. "Whatever. They sound nice." Nice is an understatement. They sound like every good thing, balled into a brilliant sunrise on a perfect summer morning.

"Oh yeah?"

"The harmonies! And who knew there was such a thing as a bass flute?"

"Look at that smile! Seems like fun."

"Uncle J!"

"Only you really know if the flute is your thing or not, but like I tell my students, you gotta release the things you're done with so you can embrace the things that bring you joy."

"I'm not done with soccer." The final exhibition match is right around the corner. And hopefully, so is my invitation to try out and maybe even join the Chargers.

CHAPTER 32

☆

Tread Lightly

Two small jumps are sometimes
better than one big leap.

I flip through the photo album, waiting on Mama
to come down for our next lesson. Even though
it's my fifth or sixth time looking at the pictures,
I still feel like I'm sneaking, eavesdropping on her
private life.

Daddy and Uncle J look the same, and Mama
looks so at home with them. Even when she is not
smiling, you can see the light radiating from her. Page
after page, I can almost hear Daddy and Uncle J rib-
bing each other. Telling jokes and teasing Mama, too.
And then there is the section of her in the pool. She's

definitely an athlete. There she is biting her first-place medal. Here she is holding a trophy.

Huh. I shiver with the inner ding you get when you realize something. This is *Mama's* photo album. There are no pictures of Daddy's soccer matches here. None of him getting trophies. This is just an album about Mama's life. Her love. Her friends. Her wins. But if these are *pictures* of her trophies, where are her *actual* trophies?

I turn and look at the bookcase. I have a whole shelf. Daddy has three shelves. Where are her shelves? I think back to that time she told Uncle J to take Daddy's trophies. Where are hers?

"What's on your mind?" I jump when she taps me on the shoulder. She studies my face, but I just shake my head.

"Nothing."

"Ready to go?"

I nod and we head out to the pool.

"Today we tread," she announces when we arrive. We hop into the water and swim to the middle, where she coaches me through the basics. I get the hang of it pretty fast, but I feel more at ease knowing the wall and the bottom are both in close reach. My heart still races at the sight of the deep water. This morning's fortune said: *Two small jumps are sometimes better than one big leap.* I totally agree. Hopefully we won't venture too deep anytime soon.

At first, I tread well from the middle, but after a while, my mind slips back to the trophies. More than once, I lose the rhythm and have to grab the wall before I sink.

"I can't tell if you're tired today, or scared of the water," Mama says, eyeing me with concern after my third grab.

I don't answer. Instead I let go of the wall, sculling and kicking, until I lose focus and grab the edge once again.

"You're doing fine, Maya, but you really need to pay attention in the water. What are you thinking about?"

I look at her, at her nose ring sparkling in the morning sun. She's so calm now, but I want to know about the trophies. If I ask her, she'll probably get mad. But if I don't, I'll definitely keep wondering. And sinking.

"Daddy didn't take his trophies when he left," I blurt out.

"No. He didn't. What made you bring that up?" She sounds more curious than upset. So far, so good.

"Is that because he's coming back soon?"

"I'm not sure why he left them. You can ask him, you know."

"I know," I say to the water. She stares at me, but I don't move or say anything else.

"What is it, Maya?" Her tone sharpens, warning me to leave it alone, but I take a deep breath and plunge ahead.

"Where are *your* trophies?"

Her face tightens. She looks away at first and then dunks underwater. When she soars back up, she brushes the water from her face, but remains quiet for a long moment. I gaze at her, holding the wall, waiting. Finally, with her eyes on the deep end, she says, "I don't know."

I frown in shock and disbelief. "You *really* don't know where they are?"

"They're from a long time ago, Maya. They're just packed away, that's all."

"But why?"

"Enough about trophies and medals from ten and fifteen years ago. The world does not revolve around trophies and awards! That's all in the past. That was then, this is now." We lock eyes. Everything is silent except the ripples of the water. Even the birds seem to be listening.

"Fine!" I say. It isn't, but I knew it would go this way.

Neither of us moves at first. Finally she sighs, softening. "Someone needs to stop stalling. No more hanging out on walls."

"I like it here," I mumble.

"No you don't," she chuckles. "No one likes being stuck on the side."

If Chaos were here, he'd say I'm stuck in Plain Janeville on the side of the pool. He'd be right.

"Let's try again. Your technique is fine—you just need to build your confidence. And concentrate."

Slowly I release the wall and tread again. Without all the questions swirling inside, it goes much smoother this time.

"You're looking really good!" I can tell she means it, too.

"Let's rest and I'll time you when you go again. But next time we come, no chitchat," she warns. "We're going into the deep."

⭐

CHAPTER 33

Too Deep

**Sometimes the thing that scares
you is the best thing for you.**

"Alright, Miss Maya," Mama says after we finish warming up in the pool. "Today's the day."

I look away from her. My sour face does not match her bright and cheerful one, and I don't want to meet her eyes. It's deep water day and it feels like a bad idea. I'm not sure I should be here at all. Yesterday was the last session of camp before the big exhibition this weekend. I did okay, but maybe not my best.

How do you find the balance between trying too hard and not hard enough? The exhibition is a big deal. It's my last shot at making a good impression on the Chargers. I should be doing soccer drills and studying games over the next two days, not splashing around in the pool.

But deep down, I know my bad mood isn't really about soccer. I'm still scared of the deep. Somehow I guess that's supposed to be a good thing? Today my fortune said: *Sometimes the thing that scares you is the best thing for you.* I'm not so sure about that.

"I know that look."

I refuse to meet her eye. "Why can't I just start from the wall?"

"Because being comfortable in the water means you can start from anywhere. You'll jump into the deep and tread just like you tread from the middle."

I huff and fold my arms across my body.

"I'll be right there. You won't be alone."

I stand at the three-feet wall, picturing myself in water more than twice as high. It seems impossible. On land, the worse that could happen is I'd mess up a play. *Or my chance at being a Charger.* I tighten my arms.

Mama claps out a cheer. "Let's go, Maya, let's go."

"Mama, don't!" I glare at the water as my cheeks get hot.

She sighs and goes for calm again, instead of matching my fire. "You can do this, Maya. I know you can." She lowers her voice, getting closer to me. "What if we go past the middle, but not all the way to the end?"

I shake my head.

"What are you afraid of?"

I think but I don't say, everything. *You and Daddy staying apart. Never being a Charger after all. Forever playing my flute on Quiet Mode. Never getting a green bracelet.* Deep down, I'm afraid nothing will be the way I really want it to be. I shrug, keeping all my Deep Downs to myself.

"I don't know. It's just too deep."

Mama nods. "I get it."

"No you don't!"

"We all have something we're afraid of," she says.

I steal a look at her, then put my eyes back on the water.

"Sometimes it's hard to face the truth. It took me a long time to face the fact that I haven't been happy."

New questions swirl, and I let them churn around for a long minute before I am brave enough to ask, "Is it because of something Daddy did? Is that why you wanted to try separation?"

"No. It's nothing he did wrong. When you were born, I stopped doing some things I really loved."

"Like swimming?"

She nods.

"Because of me?"

"No, no, no. Because of *me*. I was young. Lots of things changed, and I wasn't ready for all the changes. At first I pretended it was no big deal. I thought ignoring how I felt would make my new life easier, but it didn't. And one day, pretending things were fine just became too hard. So, I wanted some time on my own to figure out the truth. Does that make sense?"

I nod.

We're quiet again.

"Well," she says finally, "I didn't mean for us to get all . . . *deep*!" She winks.

"Mama!" I groan. "Please leave the bad jokes to Daddy!"

"Okay, okay. You don't have to rush into the deep end if you're not ready, Maya. I know you can do it, but when you try is up to you."

CHAPTER 34

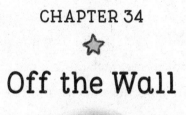

Off the Wall

Conquer your fears, or they will
conquer you.

This morning's spin of the Wheel of Fortunes landed on *Conquer your fears, or they will conquer you.* I thought it was a pep talk at first, but now, sitting here with my legs dangling in the shallow water for the second day in a row, it feels more like a warning. I'm still not ready to just jump into the deep end, whether Mama's there or not. But the longer I sit here, the worse I feel. My fear is only growing.

Mama calls out to me from the water. "This is all that's left between you and green." I shake my head. That doesn't help. Nothing's gonna help except doing it.

I slide in, push off the wall, and swim, but I am not relaxed. With each stroke, I'm not getting enough air, which makes me feel more and more nervous. When I finally pass the middle and get close enough to the deep, I just do it: I pull my knees up and tread water.

Not a good idea. It's a struggle. Nothing's in sync. I bob, sputter, and cough. When Mama grabs me and pulls me over to the side, I hide my face from hers and cling to the pool wall.

"Maya." She doesn't sound mad or disappointed, but I don't want to look at her.

"I can't do it," I say to the wall.

"Of course you can," she says, rubbing my back.

I stiffen, refusing to look at her.

I grab on to the nearby ladder and pull myself out of the pool.

"Wait, you're just going to stop?"

I don't answer. I trudge over to our stuff and grab my towel to dry off.

"I've never seen you do this. You never stop half-way. In your games you try until the last possible second. You always find an opening."

"This isn't soccer!" I shout. "You don't even like soccer. And I don't even care about this silly bracelet.

The exhibition is tomorrow. I need to be doing soccer drills, not wasting my time in this pool!"

"Then why are we here?" The sharp edges return. It almost feels good, fighting. It's familiar at least. And being mad at her feels better than the fear. "Tell me, Maya. If this is not what you want, why *are* we spending all these hours in the pool?"

"I don't know. What I want doesn't matter."

She pulls herself out of the water and sits on the edge, then taps the concrete for me to come, too. I take my time, but finally I sit with her and dangle my legs beside hers.

She leans over and asks, "Where's my fiya-cracker?" Then she sings the Name Game song in my ear. "Maya Maya bo-baya, Banana-fana fo-fiya, Fee-fi-mo-aya . . . Maya!"

"Mama."

"Maya Fiya-cracker. Fizzling out on the side of the pool, and so close to the Fourth of July. What a shame!" Her voice is teasing and tender at the same time. I take the world's deepest breath and let it all out before I say anything.

"Will you be sad if I don't take the swim test?"

"Me?" She sounds surprised at the question. "No. Will you?"

I shrug. "I just don't want to mess up."

"Mess what up?"

"Everything. The exhibition match is tomorrow. It's my last chance for the Chargers to notice me. I don't want to let Daddy down again like when I messed up on MVP. And then there's you. Everyone says you're like a mermaid . . . and you are! I wanted to get a green bracelet and have fun in the pool like all of my friends, but it's hard. I can't swim like you."

"First of all, you did not let Daddy down! You don't have to be like him or me. You don't have to do what we do. We love these things. What you love is up to you."

I fight back tears, but don't say anything.

"Really. If you don't want this, we go home right now and . . . I don't know. Bake a cake."

I let out a small smile. "You're not the baker, Mama."

"Exactly!" She holds my hand and massages my fingers. "I know you thought it was strange when I suggested band camp, but honestly? I just wanted you to have some time away and do your own thing."

I shake my head. "No. You wanted me to leave because Daddy was moving out."

"It was good timing, yes, but I wanted you to spend time in your own mind." She taps my forehead and leans in to whisper, "And stop playing Flicker in secret."

I gasp and stare at her with my mouth wide open. "You knew?"

"I'm your mother. It's my job to know."

"That was private," I say, blushing.

"I know. That's why I never said anything about it." She pulls my chin and we lock eyes.

"It's no fun being trapped in someone else's vision of things," she says. "I did that too long myself."

I blink as my tears finally fall.

"There's a whole world out there, Maya. I want you to live it. The world according to Maya! Not according to your daddy. Not me. You. What do *you* want?"

I swallow the lump in my throat and admit the truth. "I wanna feel good in the deep end. I wanna dive in whenever I please." I glance down at my wrist and smile. "And I wanna get rid of this annoying yellow bracelet."

Mama throws her head back and laughs. A deep belly laugh, loud enough to make the few others at the pool look over and laugh, too.

"Then let's get off this wall and get ready for green."

CHAPTER 35

✩

Seeing Red

The greatest test of courage on earth
is to bear defeat without losing heart.

"Let's go play some footballlllll!"

Parents on both sides clap and cheer. It's the third of July, so we're all feeling super festive for the holiday weekend. Whoever wins will definitely be lighting some extra sparklers. I throw a thumbs-up to Daddy. It's a scorcher, which is really tough since we're playing a doubleheader today. But no one will be holding back, especially not me. I spot two coaches in royal blue. The Chargers are here again! It's my last chance to get noticed.

We play well at first, but so do our opponents. For a while the score is tied 0–0. Then, just before half-time of game one, Angelica tussles with an opponent and gets a foul for pushing. Angelica may be pushy, but she has *never* put her hands on anyone in a soccer game. I'm sure of that. We all grumble and stand around in shock. Thankfully, the other team misses the free kick.

"Shake it off!" Coach yells to get us back in action. Soon enough, we win back the ball, and we lock in, making our way down the field. Suddenly I'm too close to my opponent's foot. I double step to avoid her, and trip, but don't fall. Just as I regain my balance and run, the other player goes down right behind me. Ref blows the whistle, and again whips out a yellow card as the girl rolls around grimacing and gripping her ankle. The yellow is for me! I stand there with my mouth wide open, too surprised to say or do anything else at first. Then the heat rises in the center of my chest.

Stay calm, stay calm, stay calm, I tell myself. I can't lose my temper in front of everyone, especially not today, but this is not fair. I know I didn't touch her. "Ref, what did I do?" His eyes shoot warnings—he's not answering any questions and I'd better not ask again. I look over to Coach for help. She waves and subs me out to cool off.

"Coach, what did I do?"

"Nothing. It wasn't your fault the player went down. It was just a bad call. It happens sometimes."

Well, it's "happened" twice in a row now, I think as the other team takes another free kick. It's a hot pass with both teams scrambling to win the ball. Their striker comes out on top. Then, with perfect control, she turns and shoots while we all watch in horror. Just like that, we're down 0–1. I groan.

"Don't worry about it, Maya," says Priyanka, one of my teammates, patting me on the back. I look over at Daddy. He winks and gives me a thumbs-up, so I take a deep breath and try to let it go.

Once halftime is over, Coach sends me back out. Finally, we score and tie the game 1–1. Before we lose it running and screaming all over the field, she yells at us to "Stay in the zone!" We keep it together, somehow, and both teams give it their all. Our side hustles, finally gains possession, and soon Ginger passes it over to me.

Immediately someone shouts, "Man on!" Not one,

but two players pressure me. Before I can shake them loose, one intercepts the ball and jets away. I dash after her, and as soon as we're even, I slide tackle to clear the ball and give our side a chance to win it back.

As the ball flies, we both spill to the ground, and another whistle blows. I look around just in time to see the ref point and pull out a yellow card. I look left and right to see who was guilty of a foul and realize, as he storms closer, he is pointing at me. Again! Another yellow? That's bad. Really bad. Two yellows equal red. I shake my head, refusing to believe it. But sure enough, in what feels like slow motion, the ref turns away and then rips out a red card and holds it high above his head.

"Noooo!" I yell at the top of my lungs. I stand there, balling my fists, screaming, "What did I do?" Ref, unmoved, keeps the red card high in the sky, showing everyone I'm out, out, out.

I run to the bench, plop down, and burst into tears. A red card means I have to miss the rest of this game *and* the next one, too. The last two games of camp. A red card means I'm done.

Goodbye, exhibition.

Goodbye, Chargers.

CHAPTER 36

⭐

The Real MVP

Look ahead for a fresh start.

I let the tears fall. I can't believe this is how it all ends.

"Chin up, MJ!" Daddy calls over to me.

I nod and try to calm down. There's a funny feeling in the pit of my stomach, but I don't know what it means. I just know I didn't deserve that red card. Coach Jayme tells me not to worry, that the clubs recognize strong players and they've seen me shine more than once already. I stew a little while longer, but when I look over at Daddy, he's still smiling as always, watching "the beautiful game."

Eventually, I settle in to watch, too. I study the

field and try to see it through Daddy's eyes. I've never really had a chance to just watch my friends play. To be honest, I cringe. More than once. We look bad. Almost as if we've forgotten how to play.

We're hardly moving the ball, and the other team is making good shots on goal. Thank goodness for Jackie, our goalkeeper. She is saving every shot. Even Angelica looks like she's not sure which way to run.

"What are they doing?" I throw my hands up.

Coach keeps her eyes on the field.

"They're scared!" I say.

"What's that?"

"They're giving up because of those bad calls. That's not right. They shouldn't give up! There's still so much time left!"

"Well. Here they come for a water break. Why don't you tell them?"

"Me?" I ask.

She nods and says simply, "You."

My teammates hurry to the sidelines, grasping for water and sports drinks. Coach wastes no time.

"Drink up! But listen up, too. We have less than two minutes, and Maya has something to say."

I blink, shocked at the sudden spotlight. But then I look around at everyone. Frizzy hair and sweat, scratches on legs. They're drinking water or dousing it on their necks, staring at me, waiting for my announcement. I remember the huddle from the first exhibition match. When they all looked determined, with smiles waiting in their cheeks. Those smiles are nowhere to be found right now, but I know they can't be far. Daddy would say we have a chance to change poison into medicine.

"I collect fortunes from fortune cookies. It's one of my favorite things." I pause, suddenly picturing our last family game night. I try to ignore the lump growing in my throat. Ginger nods at me to keep going. I swallow hard and try again. "I read fortunes every day for good luck. This morning my fortune said, *Look ahead for a fresh start.*"

"I didn't get it at first, but I do now. I got that red card and I sat here and cried. I was devastated, but it's already over. What I'm trying to say is, we shouldn't lose this game because we're still mad at something in the past. We gotta make a fresh start."

"Time," Coach says, pointing at her watch. Water break is almost done.

"Yes!" I say, remembering the most important part. "One thing I know for sure, if there's time left on the clock, there's still time to win."

"She's right," says Angelica. "We played those five-minute games just the other day."

"Don't remind me!" Erica moans. A giggle ripples through the group. Everyone remembers that day. We were so tired by the end.

"We scored goals almost every game!" says Queenie.

"So we all know there's still enough time. I *really* wish I could play, but when this water break is up, there's at least ten minutes left," I say, pointing to the clock. "That's basically two whole games! Let's show that ref and everyone, this is *our* field!" I shout.

"Yeah!" they shout back.

Ginger backs away from the group, drops down into a ninja stance, and yells out, "Let's go play some footballlllll!" A roar lifts from the crowd as parents cheer and clap, and the team stampedes back to the field. Without me.

Ginger skips ahead a few steps, then turns to me just long enough to say, "No matter what, my BFF is the real MVP."

CHAPTER 37

It's Bananas

Listen to your gut. It knows you best.

"Two big wins!!" Daddy shouts as he starts the Jeep. It's his turn to take us for ice cream. We complain about the ref all the way there and back until we take Ginger and Angelica home. It's fun, but I'm relieved when finally it's just me and Daddy back at "his" place.

He sets out tuna salad sandwiches on homemade bread. Except for the music streaming in the background, we inhale them in silence. I'm glad. I'm feeling too many things at once. I'm happy we won, and disappointed I didn't get to play. I definitely won't be a Charger now. I'm still in shock about that. But there's also something else. Something I don't know how to put into words.

"What'll it be now?" he asks when our plates are clean. I can tell he wants to know if I'm ready to talk about it. I'm not.

"Game time!" I shout.

"Only if you're ready to lose!"

I grab Bananagrams from the bookcase, and I can't help but notice how empty the shelves are. No books. No trophies. *Trophies.* I shiver at the inner ding, remembering.

"Daddy, why didn't you bring any trophies here?"

"I did. I brought one." He points to my participation trophy sitting across the room. I never even noticed it was missing from the house. Nameless trophy number eight. Seeing it makes me feel bad all over again. I had hoped for something totally different that day, just like I had hoped for something totally different today. This hasn't been my year for soccer after all.

"Why did you bring that one? It doesn't mean anything."

"It means something to me. And I'm sad I wasn't there when you received it. It reminds me of my favorite daughter and my favorite sport."

"But what about *your* trophies?"

He seems to think about this for a while.

"I didn't take everything important to me. Besides, I'm not sure if I'll keep all those trophies."

"Really? But you love them."

"I love my family more. I love what the trophies represented. Soccer was my whole life for a long time. Maybe too long. But that's the past. I love that *you* love it now, though."

My stomach lurches. The same feeling I had earlier when I knew I was done at the exhibition. *I love every minute!*

"Soccer's been tough lately, huh?" he asks when I don't say anything. "What do you think about it all? Still having a *ball*?" He stresses *ball* to let me know he means the pun.

"Daddy," I groan. He snickers.

"I know I'm supposed to wait until the closing banquet, but . . ."

Suddenly I'm nervous. He's going to pop the big question. But I don't want him to ask it, because for the first time, I don't know what to say.

"Are you in for next season?"

I know exactly what I'm *supposed* to say. *Yes! Let's go play some footballlll!* But this time, nothing comes out. I *want* to say it. I want his eyes to light up knowing that we have another season to look forward to together. Instead, I stare at the bulging, banana-shaped pouch, and tell the truth. My Deep Down.

"I don't know."

Silence stretches on between us, and I am afraid to meet his eyes. I want to apologize. To explain why I don't know. But I'm not sure if I really get it myself. Maybe I'm afraid to say yes because I think the Chargers are going to say no. Or maybe it's the lean. I don't lean on the way to the field. Like Mama does. When we go to the pool, she leans forward like she wants to hurry up and get there. Angelica does that, too. When she gets near the soccer field, she leans every time. When Daddy comes to the field, he leans. They can't wait. It's their favorite thing.

"I get it," he says finally. "It's been a rough couple of months."

"They might not even want me on their team."

"The Chargers? All good coaches recognize good ballers. If that's what you're worried about, you can relax."

"I was mad about that red card. But I sort of liked watching, too."

"Oh yeah?"

"I pretended I was you. Like I was watching the

game through your eyes."

"Maybe you want to be a soccer coach?"

"Daddy . . ."

I unzip the Bananagrams pouch and dump out the tiles.

"Babygirl, you know I love soccer and you know I love you more than anything. If you're not a Charger for whatever reason, I'll love you just the same."

I nod.

"What if we just go to the closing banquet in a few days, with no expectations," he says. "Certainly the food won't be any good."

We both snicker at that.

"We'll just enjoy the ceremony and figure out what to do about next season when the time comes. Deal?"

"Deal."

"Good. No pressure."

"You're the one who's about to feel this pressure when you *lose*!" I say with extra mustard so he knows I mean business.

"Fat chance! Ready?" he asks, pointing to the tiles between us.

"Ready! Twenty-one a piece. Count 'em out! Let's go!"

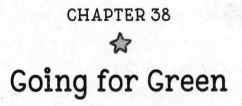

CHAPTER 38

Going for Green

If you want the rainbow, you have
to tolerate the rain.

I'm in the Cave, playing arpeggios on Quiet Mode. I know I don't have to play quietly anymore, but the soft, windy sound is calming, and the up-and-down rhythm gives the butterflies in my stomach something else to do. We're leaving for the swim test any minute now.

It will only take five minutes.

In a soccer game, everything can change in five minutes. A losing team can win. A winning team can lose. All the momentum can shift. I'm great on land—running, kicking, passing the ball. Water has been tougher to master.

It will only take five minutes.

What if I lose my nerve? Forget everything I've been practicing? I shake away those thoughts. I know I can do this. It will not turn out like the Golden Astro or the exhibitions. Lifeguards don't give red cards, do they? No bad calls, right?

It will only take five minutes.

If I pass, I will finally get a green bracelet. On the Fourth of July at that. My own Declaration of Independence from the shallow end. I put Flicker back in the case and listen. An eastern towhee is singing. The trills remind me of my flute, but it's nothing like a wood thrush. It's been forever since I've heard my favorite bird. I'm walking over to the Wheel to spin it for extra luck when Mama knocks and swings open my door.

"Maya? Are you almost ready?"

"Yes, ma'am."

"Why do I always catch you standing at the Wheel?"

The strangest idea comes to mind.

"Mama?"

"Maya?"

"You wanna spin?"

"Me?" Mama smiles. "Show me," she says, pointing with her chin.

I concentrate on getting green today. I spin and then close my eyes, holding on to my wish. I open them and groan.

"What's wrong? What does it say?"

"*If you want the rainbow, you have to tolerate the rain.* Yuck."

"Well, what did you want it to say?"

"I don't know. Something better."

"But that's up to you," Mama says, chuckling.

"It's not funny."

"Don't you remember when we made this? Where's the first one? Is it still here?"

I scan the Wheel until I find it, then point.

"Yes! *You have the power to write your own fortune.* Don't you remember that?"

"I remember you two liked it, but I didn't."

"Aww. You were too young. It means it's *your* life. These are just . . . suggestions. Pick something else."

I frown at her. "Just pick one?"

"Yes! Like I said before, it's the world according to Maya. You can make your own fortune." I consider this for a moment, then decide to give it a try.

"Okay . . . but don't watch."

"Okay, okay."

Mama turns her back to me while I scan the Wheel. I turn and turn it until the chopstick points exactly where I want it. I close my eyes and repeat my fortune silently three times to make sure it's locked in.

"Done," I announce.

"Well, Babygirl, this swim test won't pass itself. Let's go!"

No jolt flies through me when she says "Babygirl" this time. No quick flash of heat. Maybe it's because, even with her back to me, I can hear the smile in her voice.

We set out for the pool. Even though it's still early, it's already getting hot. No clouds to hide the sun shining on our shoulders. The whole way there, I repeat my fortune to myself. I wish I didn't feel so nervous, but at least no one will see. Everyone will be here later today, but it's usually just us in the mornings.

"Before swim meets, I was nervous, too," Mama says, breaking through my thoughts. "I did things to cheer myself up and remind myself I'm a good swimmer. The best one in my lane at least!"

"Your lane? What about the rest of the pool?"

"Well, I liked to think I was the best swimmer in the pool, but I wasn't always. Besides, the biggest competition is in here." She points to herself. "Are you at *your* best today? Or mailing it in? I can't control the rest of the pool, but I can control my lane, that's for doggone sure."

I stare at her. That's exactly how I feel when I play soccer. I can't control anyone else, but I can do my part.

"What's that on your nose?" A swirly silver nose ring adorns her whole left nostril. "Is it new?"

"Nope. Older than you! I cleaned it this morning."

"It's cool!"

"Oh yeah?" She laughs. "Thank you. I used to wear it for special occasions." She smiles at me, but I look away, embarrassed, and more nervous. We walk up to the window and check in. Lori, the lifeguard, introduces herself. Mama points to a nearby chair and stretches out.

While Lori explains the swim test, I stare at my yellow bracelet and try to block out the giggles I hear nearby. *No one is supposed to be here yet.* I shake my shoulders to lighten up. It's just a five-minute swim test, not life or death. Lori gives me one more chance to ask questions, but before I can tell her I'm fine, a loud voice rings out.

"Hey! Let's go pass a swim teeeeeeest!!"

Ginger and Angelica wave furiously from the middle of the pool. My heart soars and sinks at the same time. I'm so glad to see them, but now I have an audience. The butterflies in my stomach go full speed ahead, and I pray I don't get sick right here in front of everyone.

"Are you okay?" asks Lori when she sees me tugging my bracelet. "If you're not ready, you don't have to do this."

I glance over at Mama. She nods and gives me a thumbs-up and a big smile. I definitely want a green bracelet. Not for Mama. Not for Daddy. Not for Ginger or anyone else. Just for me. And deep down, I know I'm ready. I am no longer afraid of the deep.

I remind myself of my fortune, the one *I* chose:

Nothing can keep you from reaching your goals. Do it!

Then I turn to Lori the lifeguard and nod. "I'm ready. I'm ready to get my green!"

CHAPTER 39

☆

Fireworks

Everything will come your way.

Daddy and Uncle Jimmy come over later to celebrate my green. They both come bearing gifts. I open Daddy's first.

"Battleship?"

"We needed a new *B* game, and you can't go wrong with classics. Don't worry, you'll get used to saying 'You sunk my battleship'!"

"You mean *you'll* get used to saying it. You sound like you already are."

We laugh as I unwrap the next box. I open the top to reveal Daddy's specialty cake—red velvet. It's a thing of beauty. Who knew buttermilk and vinegar could taste so good in cakes and icing? I moan in delight.

"Can we eat it now?"

"Let's see what your uncle brought, first."

"I brought perfection, of course. Start with this one." Uncle J points to a small brown box. I tear it open and pull out a white T-shirt. It says *I love music* with a big red heart.

"Oh! Is this what they looked like? The *I love New York* shirts?"

"Yes, ma'am. But you get the real deal since we finally know the flute is not just your *friend*."

"Thanks, Uncle J." I hug him, blushing. Now that soccer camp is done, we'll be doing flute lessons together starting next week.

"Of course! This is like your official band jersey. That means we have to get your name or nickname on the back. What'll it be?"

I think for a second. Nobody calls me *Maya* except people who don't know me very well, and Mama. But I like it when she says my name now. When I am really listening, it sounds like a love song.

"Well, my name is Maya. Maya *Jazzmine. MJ* for short. Let's go with *MJ*."

"That's my favorite niece right there!" Uncle J

grabs me and gives me another big squeeze. "Consider it done! Last but not least . . ." He points to another small box. This one is sort of wrapped, covered with newspaper, but I know what it is. I can already smell the sweet deliciousness. I tear off the paper and laugh. Daddy snorts.

"Really, Jimmy? Is that what you brought my child? Store-bought rings of sugar?"

"Your red velvet cake does get a ten out of ten. But Krispy Kreme glazed, HOT NOW, will always get an eleven. Stop playing!" He pops Daddy in the chest. "Let's eat. Them thangs still warm!"

"I can't believe it. You just mad 'cause it's the Fourth of July and we didn't plan another Grill-Off for today."

"Name the time and place, sir. Me and my grill *and my barbecue sauce* will be right there to show you how it's done. Again."

We're all cracking up, until Daddy breaks the spell.

"Leah?" He says her name softly, and we all quiet down. "What do you think?"

Mama doesn't say anything at first. We wait, as still as statues. "Does this mean you're expecting me to make my potato salad again this summer?" she asks finally. I clap when I see the smile easing from her lips.

"Yes!" I shout. "Please, Mama? Please?"

"Why is everyone asking me?"

"Come on now, sis," says Uncle J.

"Is this just about another Grill-Off . . . or something else?" Mama asks, her eyes on Daddy.

I look down then, afraid of what might happen next. She sighs, pulls out a chair, and sits at the kitchen table, now covered with treats and wrappings. We all take seats with her.

"The truth?"

Daddy reaches for her hand. She reaches back and takes a deep breath while I hold mine.

"I've loved you since high school, Mathew Jenkins." She looks at me. "Did you know we called him *MJ* for short?"

"No!"

"But in college we had to switch to *Mat* because it was more grown-up." She turns back to him. "I've realized a lot in the past month. Between college and now, I put a little too much of myself in storage, hidden away with the trophies I didn't want to see anymore. I'm going to need a little more time and maybe a little bit of help to finish . . . unpacking. Maybe the two of us can go talk to someone and unpack things together?"

Mama tells you a lot in looks, touches, and small movements, and the light in her eyes gives it all away. She's saying yes to a Grill-Off! And yes, they're going to try to end the separation! All eyes bounce to Daddy. He smiles a huge smile, all the way from his toes. But when he speaks, he's quiet. Not a rumbling thunder. A sweet quiet. Joy.

"You got it."

"Alright, enough fireworks inside!" shouts Uncle J. "It's the Fourth of July. Let's go find some fireworks *outside* like everybody else. Grab Flicker, MJ. We're all going to the park."

CHAPTER 40

⭐

According to Maya

The respect of influential people
will soon be yours.

Daddy drives me to the camp's closing banquet. This isn't a regular banquet, so there is no cold pizza or rec center auditorium. But we do have hot dogs and burgers outside, under white tents.

"Even Jimmy coulda done better than these jokers," says Daddy, chomping into a dry burger. Look!" He points to the bottles of barbecue sauce on every table. "They know it, too. But I guess these will do."

There is no closing video, but they do play pop songs while we eat. Up front, several medals are laid out across the head table. They are all the same size but different colors. Participation medals. *I wonder what color I'll get?*

Once we're just about done eating, Coach Jayme taps the mic and the music fades out. "Priyanka, will you please come forward?" Pri gasps, looking around at us, surprised and confused like everybody else. She half walks and half jogs to the front, then turns to stare at us while we all stare back. I don't think any of us ever had a closing ceremony work quite this way before. No one knows what's next.

While Priyanka stands there looking ready to run away, Coach begins to list all the awesome things she did during camp: leading us in stretches, helping to make sure everyone was hydrated, and comforting anyone who was having a hard time. In the end, Coach names Priyanka the *Quiet Warrior* and puts a purple medal around her neck. We all say "Ooooh" and clap as she nods and blushes and runs back to her seat.

Queenie is next. Coach goes on this way, calling each player first, then making her stand there in front of us, while praising her for all the great things she did during camp. We've never heard this many words from Coach on one day before, but everyone gets her own medal for exactly what she contributed.

By the time she finishes Angelica, the *Super Striker*, there are just two of us left. Ginger and me. Our fingers touch, overlapping with each other, waiting to see who's next. Why do I feel nervous? I squeeze her hand. She squeezes back.

"Ginger! Come on up!" Ginger looks at me and winks, then skips up to the front. Coach says many of the same things we heard at the Astros closing banquet. How she is skilled, calm, and flexible. Coach sums it all up, calling Ginger the *Most Versatile Player*. We hoot and clap as she blushes her way back down the aisle. When she sits down smiling, green medal around her neck, I smile back. A big one. No jealousy in my heart this time. I really am happy for her. Once again, she is MVP.

"Last, but certainly not least, MJ." Coach waves me up to the front, and even though I knew it was my turn, I can barely move from the flutters in my stomach. Daddy whoops, shame-free, clapping me up to the front.

"Well, MJ," Coach starts, "it's been a long road. That first day was a little shaky." I look down, but nod as everyone snickers. "It was clear you thought you had something to prove. And you did. You are a star player. But as we all know, teamwork is not about being a soloist. It's about how we all play together." I nod again, looking up now, watching teammates and parents nod, too. "You found a lovely groove with your teammates just in time for that red card." My cheeks burn, but I giggle as everyone groans and yells things like "Come on, Coach!"

"That was a tough day. But I learned the most about you in that moment. Even though your heart was broken, you gave both pieces, the whole thing, right back to the team. Whether on the field or off, you always had a fighting spirit. You were tenacious. You never, ever gave up. Everyone join me as I congratulate our *Tenacious Tiger*."

Coach slips the shiny blue medal around my neck, and I think I might float away. I clap along with everyone else, laughing and smiling all the way from my toes. I dash back to Daddy, who is beaming as bright as two sunshines, and rub my nose on his.

After the ceremony, we head to the exhibit tables to meet the club coaches and get swag from each of the teams.

"Anybody you wanna visit first?" Daddy asks. I know his mind is on the Chargers. Mine too. I can't miss the royal blue and gold table, but I'm not ready to go there. Not yet. I shake my head no and squeeze his hand.

There are several teams here, each with their own decorated tables. Cheerful coaches and team parents stand near each one, waving us closer and answering questions. We go table by table, nodding and picking up brochures. The closer we get to the Chargers, the more the butterflies swirl.

We save them for last, and by the time we approach their table, we're loaded down with sports bottles, key chains, and bags. The coach stands up and extends his hand to me.

"Nice medal you've got there. It's the right color and everything."

"Thanks." I smile, glancing down at it.

"Maya, right?"

"Yes! *MJ* for short. How'd you know?"

"We've been out here a couple times. I've seen you playing. You looked great out there. You and your friends had a nice triad going. Is this camp your first time playing together?"

"No, we were all Astros."

"It shows. Bummer on that red card. Between you and me, that wasn't a great call. But you shook it off and even helped motivate your team. We like to see that in a player."

I nod and smile and say "Thank you," thinking that's it. But he continues.

"Staying focused and optimistic, and getting everyone fired up! That's real leadership under pressure. Plus your skill with the ball? Definitely Charger material. No guarantees, but we'd love to have you try out for our team! Whaddya say?"

My breath catches. I've been waiting to hear this question, this exact one, since the beginning of the summer. Really since the beginning of soccer this year. My heart tries to leap from my chest.

I break eye contact with the coach and look up at Daddy. He looks pleased as punch, stroking his beardless chin, listening. I wait to see if he'll say anything, but he shakes his head. "It's up to you, MJ," he says softly behind his hand.

Coach points to the list—where everyone has signed up for tryouts. I skim the names. Angelica's is high on the page, and then right underneath is Ginger's. In what seems like slow motion, Coach holds the pen out to me.

If you're not a Charger for whatever reason, I'll love you just the same, Daddy had said. I picture Uncle J, looking just like him, telling me to listen better, especially to myself. And then Mama, who found her smile again because she stopped pretending her feelings didn't matter. *What do you want?* she'd asked. She told me to create my own fortune – my own world. *The world according to Maya! Not Daddy. Not me. You.*

Deep down, I knew the answer. I've always known. It's Daddy I love, not soccer. I only like soccer as a friend. I swallow the lump in my throat and squeeze Daddy's hand as I wave away the pen.

"Thanks for inviting me to try out, Coach. It was my goal all year to have a chance to make your team. But . . . I think this is my last time playing soccer for a while." Daddy exhales quietly and squeezes my hand back.

Coach nods and looks truly disappointed. I believe him when he says, "I'm sorry to hear that. Tryouts are next week. You can change your mind anytime between now and the first day, and we'd love it."

I nod, shake his hand again, and say "Thank you." I'm sad saying goodbye to soccer, but I know I won't be changing my mind.

"Ready?" Daddy asks as we turn and head toward the car.

"Ready."

⭐

CHAPTER 41

Polo!

Investigate new possibilities with
friends. Now is the time!

I shake my shoulders and shimmy around the house to "Vengo Caliente" by Sonora Carruseles. Mama throws her head back and laughs and even dances with me for a little while, dusting off her old moves. When the doorbell rings, I run to let Ginger in. She laughs and wiggles, getting in on the fun, too. Mama fusses at us to make sure we agree to wear sunscreen and drink water at the pool because it's July in Georgia and it's hot!

"You should come, too, Mama."

"Oh yeah? Why is that?"

"It's my one-week-aversery of passing my swim test, and even better, it's National Swimming Pool Day!"

"There's no such thing."

"It is! Ask Chaos."

"And tell me again, the Grill-Off with your Daddy and Jimmy is supposed to be what holiday?"

"The first Sunday in August. American Family Day! It's real, Mama! Look it up!"

"Girl, get out of here. Have fun, baby," she says, planting a loud kiss on my cheek.

I've been in the deep end almost every day since I passed the test, but only in the mornings. It's my first time back for Marco Madness. When we arrive at the pool, Ginger holds her wrist over the scanner, and Ms. Shae, who has silver nails now, waves her in. When she chirps my bracelet, she calls my whole name, "Maya J. Jenkins?"

"*MJ* for short."

"I remember you!" She leans in closer. "Congratulations on green! Have fun!" She waves with all ten fingers, and together Ginger and I skip to the poolside. Everyone's here. Even for Marco Madness, it seems super-duper crowded. Maybe because school starts back in a few weeks. We toss our stuff on one of the two or three chairs left.

"Last one in is a rotten egg!" yells Angelica, running past us and flying into a magnificent cannonball. We strip down to our suits as fast as we can.

"No, last one in is Marcooo!" shouts Chaos just as he belly flops right into the middle of the pool.

We hurry to spray each other with sunscreen, as kids start screaming and hollering, "NOT IT! NOT IT!" and "Polo! Not it!" They leap into the pool left and right from all sides. No one nearby is still dry.

"Hurry up!" yells Ginger, her voice rising. "We're going to be IT!" One look at her smile and I know that she isn't worried about being IT. But am I? I think back to the first time I saw the new pool. How deep the deep end seemed. I couldn't have imagined myself doing what I'm thinking of doing right now.

I've never seen one in person, but wood thrushes are my favorite bird of all time. I know hearing one doesn't mean good luck, not exactly. But they sound lucky. Cheerful, like my favorite instrument. When I finally heard one singing early this morning, I knew today would be special. But I didn't know why until right this second.

Chaos waves us on. "MJ, Ginger, hurry!" he yells, pointing behind us. We turn to see the three Jackson brothers rushing from the entrance. They're the only other kids still out of the pool.

"Ready?" Ginger yells with one foot cocked to run.

I smile.

"I've been thinking. We should celebrate National Swimming Pool Day."

"Um, MJ . . ."

I strike a Superman pose, legs spread, fists on my hips, and announce, "Today's fortune: *Investigate new possibilities with friends. Now is the time!*"

"Whaaaattt?" screams Ginger, figuring out my idea.

"Let's go!"

And with that, she grabs my hand and we take off. Together we dash to the edge of the pool, and then we leap with all our might. Up, up, up we fly, and I scream at the top of my lungs, "MARCO!" And *whoosh*! We splash! Down, down, down until we tap the bottom. We push back up, soaring straight to the top. As soon as I clear the surface, I hear cheers and claps. I brush the water off my face and look over to see Ginger doing the same.

"Ready?" I ask.

"Ready!"

Treading water, I throw my head back, hands cupped around my mouth, shame-free, then take a deep breath and let it rip. "Let's get ready to rumbllllllle!" dragging the *l* for extra drama. I cover my eyes with big fanfare and yell again for all to hear, "MARCO!"

Smiling deep down, all the way from my toes.

Acknowledgments

They say sophomore novels can be difficult, and that was certainly the case with this one. I wrote the first draft during the first year of the COVID-19 pandemic, and by the time I finished the last paragraph, I felt I was in a world of trouble. It was nothing close to the story I'd imagined it would be. I was exhausted and out of ideas. I knew it would get there—somewhere—eventually, but the when, where, and how were complete unknowns.

Anyone who publishes a book knows it's the ultimate group project. It's truly a team effort. *Maya* is out in the world today thanks to the love, encouragement, and support of countless people. Chief among them is my first editor, Margaret Raymo, who had "no doubt I'd get there" when "there" was still a million miles away. Thank you, Margaret. With your meaningful feedback and helpful probes, I discovered a path forward.

Thank you to Chris Negron and Toni Bellon, who read early versions of *Maya*, and to Rey, Jr., for chatting me up about banquets, awards, and all that jazz. Thanks also to my soccer SMEs: Thad "Get Low" Harp, Rich Smith (with Asher and Isaiah), and the dynamic duo, Kirah and Gibbzy. I appreciate your careful reading and notes about what to improve.

I treasure the wisdom, fellowship, and accountability of #the21ders and #22debuts, especially: Kate Albus, Shakirah Bourne, Yvette Clark, Erica George, Chrystal D. Giles, Anne-Sophie Jouhanneau, Emma Kress, Sylvia Liu, Naila Moira, Erik Jon Slangerup, and Alysa Wishingrad. Thank you all for lending your precious resources, including time, knowledge, and companionship. Through conversations, recommendations, or just showing up week by week, you helped me cross the finish line.

Endless gratitude to my agent, Danielle Chiotti, who was always ready with a compassionate ear and deft questions, and most of all, the ability to withhold laughs and scorn at zero drafts.

The characters Daddy and Uncle Jimmy were inspired by real-life identical twins: Daddy and DNA Daddy Uncle Arnsel. Their witty banter with each other and all of their siblings formed the soundtrack of my childhood. Thank you both for the fun memories and inspiration.

Thank you so much to Blue, my BFF and partner in crime, and my big sister, cousin, and business partner, Dr. (Little) Cherry, who is always there in big ways and small. Thank you to Christina Soontornvat, the best mentor a new author could ask for. And to my Byakuren, Dalia Chetty, Kimiko Reed, and Michele Hostler, I appreciate you always.

Praises to all of my family and friends, including those who have passed on. You are never far.

Thank you to the whole team at HarperCollins and Versify. Special thanks to Weslie Turner, Ciera Burch, Monica Perez, Mary Magrisso, Heather Tamarkin, and Jen Strada for all of your work behind the scenes.

Thanks to Celeste Knudsen for *Maya*'s brilliant cover design and to Sawyer Cloud for the lovely illustration. It's nothing short of a miracle seeing the character you imagined come to life!

Thanks also to Ro Romanello, Anna Ravenelle, and Lisa Disarro for publicity and marketing, and helping readers find *Maya*.

Most of all, deep gratitude to Amy Cloud for your warmth and for your detailed and encouraging editing. Thank you so much for helping me to see that sometimes, our manuscripts just need a little fairy dust.